Louisa Heaton is a married mother of four—including a set of twins—and lives on an island in Hampshire. When not wrangling her children, husband or countless animals, she can often be found walking her dogs along the beach, muttering to herself as she works out plot points. In her spare time she reads a lot and crochets. Usually when she ought to be doing something else!

Also by Louisa Heaton

Seven Nights with Her Ex
Christmas with the Single Dad
Reunited by Their Pregnancy Surprise
Their Double Baby Gift
Pregnant with His Royal Twins
A Child to Heal Them
Saving the Single Dad Doc
Their Unexpected Babies
The Prince's Cinderella Doc
Pregnant by the Single Dad Doc

Discover more at millsandboon.co.uk.

HEALED BY
HIS SECRET BABY

LOUISA HEATON

MILLS & BOON

Published in Great Britain 2020
by Mills & Boon, an imprint of HarperCollins*Publishers*
1 London Bridge Street, London, SE1 9GF

© 2020 Louisa Heaton

ISBN: 978-0-263-08774-1

MIX
Paper from
responsible sources
FSC® C007454

This book is produced from independently certified FSC™ paper
to ensure responsible forest management.
For more information visit www.harpercollins.co.uk/green.

Printed and bound in Great Britain
by CPI Group (UK) Ltd, Croydon, CR0 4YY

For all the lovely staff at Staunton. xxx

CHAPTER ONE

Hey, you.

So, this is it. My final wish. And I'm sorry I'm asking you to do this, but I truly have no one else. You're the only one I trust, and you've always been there for me, and now I'm asking you to be there again. But this time it's for Tori and that way you can't say no!

I never told her father. You know why, and it was the right thing to do at the time, but as I get closer to going I can't help but think of my darling little girl having no one in the world she's related to. I've been there. I've done that. And it's a lonely place. She'll have you, her godmother, but...she has a father out there and he could be amazing!

So, I'm tasking you with this. Find him. His name is Cole Branagh and he's a doctor. A GP. And if he's a doctor then surely he cares about people? I'm hoping he has a good heart. I'm hoping he can be everything she needs.

I want you to find him, and if you think he's a good man then let him know about Tori.

I need you to find her daddy.

I know you'll make the right decisions.
Much love to you, always and for ever,
Skye xxx

LANE PUT DOWN the note and exclaimed, 'Why are you making me do this?'

She went to scrunch it up in frustration but then stopped, thought better of it, and instead stared with defeat at the Liberty Point Surgery, a small general practice nestled in the village of Bourton-on-the-Water. As if just staring at the building long enough would make this whole sorry mess disappear.

He was in there. Cole Branagh.

Dr Cole Branagh.

The man who'd slept with her best friend when he really ought to have known better than to take advantage of a woman whose inhibitions were in question because of her alcohol intake.

Lane knew *exactly* what type of man he'd be. A charmer. A user of women. The type to hang around in bars looking for lonely easy pickings. This Cole Branagh bloke had got *exactly* what he wanted from Skye and nothing more.

Just like Simon.

And here she was, sitting in her car, feeling trepidation about going in there because a man like that wouldn't want to know about his dead one-night stands, or babies they didn't know they'd fathered. Men like that didn't care.

Lane had uprooted her own life just to find this slime ball and have her theories proved right! Surely this was going to be a waste of time? Skye had told Lane all she needed to know about this Cole Branagh!

It had been quite easy to find him on the internet. Liberty Point Surgery's website helpfully had a staff page with a smiling photo of each member of staff and a short paragraph explaining a bit about who they were. Probably to make them seem human.

Who would want to have a go at medical receptionist Mary when they knew she knitted hats for the preemie babies up at St Luke's?

Cole was the only one who had no photo and his paragraph was missing. There was just his name and a list of his qualifications.

Dr Cole Branagh, BM, MRCGP, DGM, DFFP, DRCOG

Such an impressive array of letters. She'd had to look them up to see what they meant. Bachelor of Medicine. Member of the Royal College of General Practitioners. Diploma in Geriatric Medicine. Diploma of the Faculty of Family Planning. Diploma of the Royal College of Obstetrics and Gynaecologists...

She'd laughed cynically at those last two. This man who knew so much about the best way to have a baby, was a man who had *no idea* he had an eight-month-old daughter. Wasn't *that* ironic?

Sighing with irritation, she folded Skye's letter and slipped it back into her bag as she stared once more at the surgery building, delaying for just a few more moments. It looked quite nice, as surgeries went. Modern. Redbrick. It even had hanging baskets filled with flowers in glorious pinks and greens.

She'd been lucky they'd needed a temporary healthcare assistant. Lane had registered with an agency in order to get the post there and her mum had stepped in to babysit

Tori whilst she discovered if this Dr Branagh could be trusted to know that he had a child.

She flipped down the visor to see the photo she'd tucked there. It was of her and Skye. Tori's mother was blowing out the candles on a birthday cake, with one arm around Lane, wearing a silly paper party hat. It had been taken just one year away from a diagnosis that would change everything.

'I can't believe you're making me do this, Skye,' she said out loud. 'Who am I to be judge and jury?'

You're Tori's legal guardian, that's who. It was as if Skye's voice came to her. *You made me a promise. On my deathbed. You can't break it!* She could almost hear the devilish chuckle in her friend's voice.

No. She wouldn't break it. She'd sworn it, holding Skye's hands, squeezing them tight as her best friend in the whole wide world had taken her final breaths.

She'd almost lost herself afterwards. The intense grief had pulled her towards an unimaginable darkness.

She and Skye had been friends for ever. Since infants' school. Skye had seemed strange to Lane at first. Someone without a mum? Or a dad? But they had bonded instantly and stuck by each other's side through everything.

Until the very end.

Only baby Tori had kept Lane going. Going through the courts to get official guardianship. The little girl laughed and smiled just like her mummy! Tori was all she had left of Skye. And now she had to decide if some man—*whom she didn't even know!*—could be a father to that precious little girl. That some sleazeball from a bar would have to be in their lives.

It wasn't fair.

She hated him already. But Skye, bless her heart, had

thought that he deserved a chance to know his daughter. That he deserved a chance to show that he could be a good man and a good father.

'He'd better be some kind of unbelievable saint,' she said out loud to the photo. 'That's all I'm saying.'

Five minutes later, she was walking inside the surgery, headache brewing, with her backpack over her shoulder, trying to look as if she wasn't an undercover spy on a secret mission, but just an ordinary agency healthcare assistant, ready to start her new posting.

But when she got inside, she saw a crowd of people huddled around a person lying on the floor, and her instincts immediately kicked in.

She dropped her bag. 'Let me through! I can help!' she said as she barged her way through, pushing and shoving, desperate to give assistance.

Only she burst through to the front of them to see a woman lying on the floor, looking up at her with curiosity, whilst kneeling beside her was a very handsome man who had clearly been in the middle of some kind of demonstration.

'Hi,' he said, one eyebrow raised in question.

Lane glanced again at the 'patient'. A woman who seemed to be totally unhurt, with a big smile on her face. A woman who was conscious. Breathing. Absolutely fine.

She could only blush as around her one or two people chuckled. 'What—what's going on?' she stammered.

The man smiled. 'First aid demo. I'm showing our patients how to put someone into the recovery position.' He pointed at one of the walls. 'There are posters.'

She followed his finger and noticed that every wall, and even the door through which she'd walked, had a large poster on it, stating that all were welcome to attend an emergency first aid demo to be held at the surgery today. A demo that would be run by Dr Cole Branagh.

How had she not noticed? Had she been so absorbed in trying to look normal?

Lane swallowed hard and turned back to face the man who had now taken the hand of the 'patient' and was helping her gently to her feet.

Tori has his eyes.

He didn't look anything like the charming Lothario weasel she'd pictured in her head. Annoyingly, he had the audacity to be extremely handsome, and she could understand how Skye might have fallen for his charms. The females all around him seemed to be gazing at him with appreciative eyes and he clearly thrived on their attention. Their *adulation*.

He was probably used to having women throw themselves at his feet.

Well, not me, Dr Branagh.

'Right. Okay. Sorry I interrupted.' She grimaced and turned away, trying to control the heat flaming in her cheeks, and pushed back through the assembled throng to get to the reception desk, where she introduced herself in a low, embarrassed voice. 'Lane Carter...agency HCA.'

The woman on Reception was Mary, knitter of preemie hats—she recognised her from her research—and she smiled at her. 'Oh, yes, we've been expecting you. You're in Treatment Room Two. This is your card for the computer.' She passed over a temporary locum ID card that hung from an NHS lanyard. 'Let me show you where everything is.'

Cole stood in the small staff kitchenette, making himself a cup of tea. He was feeling great. The first aid demo had produced a great turn-out, with more people attending than he'd expected. He'd taught them how to deal with choking, adult CPR and baby CPR, and putting a person into the simple recovery position.

He smiled as he remembered the young woman who had interrupted his demonstration. He liked it that she'd been eager. Keen to help. And the look on her face when she'd realised it was a demo had been priceless!

As if his thoughts had summoned her, she suddenly appeared in the doorway of the kitchenette. She stopped when she saw him standing there. Just briefly. Then she came in to grab a mug out of the cupboard.

'Hello, again,' he said, holding out his hand. 'We didn't get to introduce ourselves earlier. The name's Branagh—Cole Branagh.'

Weirdly, she seemed to hesitate, as if she didn't want to shake his hand, but then she did, and smiled a greeting that wasn't quite genuine.

'Lane Carter,' she said.

He felt a little puzzled. Was she upset at being so embarrassed that morning? He didn't want her to be. Anyone could have made the same mistake.

'You're our agency HCA?'

'Yes.'

'Thank God. We certainly need you after Shelby's mad dash to Scotland to be with her father. Heart attack,' he added, just to clarify. 'Your being here will lighten the load for the nurses.'

It really would. They'd been overwhelmed since Shelby had left, having to take on her workload, too. It had been causing some real problems for the poor receptionists, who were taking the flak from disgruntled patients, because they couldn't get an appointment for weeks.

She grabbed a decaffeinated teabag from the box and popped it in her mug. 'Good. I hope I'll be of some *real* help.'

He smiled, assuming she was referring to that morning's mishap. 'I'm sure you will be. You certainly seem raring to go, and we need that around here.'

She turned from him and poured hot water into her mug. 'I always do my best.'

'Good. Well, maybe I'll see you later?'

Lane nodded. 'Definitely.'

He grabbed his own tea and left the kitchenette, feeling a little odd. Something hadn't been quite right with their conversation, and for the life of him he couldn't pinpoint what it was. Lane Carter had seemed...*tense*. Which was odd, because normally he was great at putting people at their ease.

Perhaps it was first day nerves and she just needed some time to feel comfortable?

Yes. That had to be it. She'd be fine.

He had no doubt that she would fit in very well once she got comfortable with her surroundings. And perhaps, someday, they'd find themselves hoping that she'd never leave at all.

'The name's Branagh—Cole Branagh.'

My God, did the man think he was James Bond? Did he lean on bars, drink in hand, twinkle in eye, as he said that? Charming women with his suave introduction, his bespoke suit and those twinkling blue eyes? He probably had a sports car in the car park.

He had no cares in the world at all! Here he was, living his best life, women at his feet, whilst *she* had been through the worst loss ever, had had to turn her entire life around and was now caring for *his* child, whilst he swanned about in his expensive tailored clothes and shiny shoes?

It was unfair. It was wrong.

Lane put her mug of tea down on the desk and noticed that on the screen it told her she had a patient waiting for a blood test. She pressed the button to call her in, and whilst she waited for her to arrive got out the equipment she'd need. Just a turquoise vial for the warfarin test. A needle, vacutainer, swab and tourniquet.

The patient arrived and sat down. 'You're new.'

'Yes, my name's Lane, Mrs Downing. Can you confirm your date of birth for me, please?'

Mrs Downing confirmed it, and even added her address.

'Thank you. Now, you're here to have a blood test. Do you have your yellow slip?'

The yellow slip came from the anti-coagulation clinic at the hospital, so that it would go back with the blood sample to Pathology.

'Yes, lovey, here you go. You might have a bit of a hard time of it, though. My veins aren't very good.'

Lane smiled and grabbed the tourniquet. 'Let's take a look, shall we?'

She cast her gaze over both her patient's arms and decided to pick the left, which looked more likely to give her a successful blood draw. She tied the tourniquet.

'How does that feel? Not too tight?'

'No, it's fine—you go ahead. I won't look, though.'

'As long as one of us does, hey?'

Lane smiled and palpated the patient's arm, finding the median cubital vein almost immediately. She swabbed the area and let it dry.

'Sharp scratch coming...' She inserted the needle, added the vial to the vacutainer and the blood began to flow. 'There you go. No problem.'

Mrs Downing still wasn't looking. 'Have you done it?'

'Yes. Got it first go.' She removed the needle and added a cotton swab. 'Press here for me.'

'It's done? Oh, you *are* good! You can do that again; I'll have to ask for you next time. I like all the nurses here, but the one I saw two weeks ago gave me some horrible bruises trying to find my veins. I was black and blue!'

Lane tried to give a sympathetic look but didn't want to say anything detrimental about nurses—it just wasn't right. No one tried to hurt a patient on purpose. It would have been no one's fault.

She scribbled Mrs Downing's details onto the vial and popped it into the bag with the yellow slip, then checked to make sure her patient's arm had stopped bleeding before she put on some tape to hold the wadding in place.

'Leave that on for an hour or two. No heavy lifting, okay?'

Mrs Downing smiled and winked. 'I'll give the gym a miss today, then, lovey. Am I all done?'

'You are. Have a nice day, Mrs Downing.'

'You too, lovey.'

Lane popped the blood sample into the collection box and cleaned down, ready for her next patient. He hadn't arrived yet, so she took a sip of her tea, thinking about the chick magnet in the next room.

Dr Branagh's consulting room was right next to hers. He was mere feet away. Just a wall between them. And she held a secret that would bring his well-ordered life crashing down in an instant.

Tori's arrival had made Lane change her entire life,

so she wondered if she ought to feel sorry for him? But then she decided not to. No one had ever felt sorry for *her*. Simon hadn't even considered her feelings. All he'd been able to think about was himself. His own happiness.

Well, Lane had to consider *Tori's* happiness. That poor little girl had lost her mother for ever, and she would not introduce her father into her life until she knew she could trust him not to ruin it even further. Simon, and even her own father, had taught her that when the going got tough or complicated, most men bailed out.

What if Cole was no good?

What if he was reckless?

What if he had no idea how to look after a child?

What if he walked out on Tori after only a few weeks?

What if he's married already?

That thought made her chew on a fingernail.

What if Dr Branagh had a *wife*? Lane would be causing problems for her, too. What if he already had kids? They'd have a new half-sister...

And suddenly, as if her thoughts had summoned him to her room, there he was in her doorway, stethoscope draped casually around his neck, smiling his charming disarming smile and looking at her with those gorgeous baby blues.

'Hey, do you have a moment? I need a chaperon.'

She blinked. Nodded. Looked to see if he had a ring on his left hand. He didn't.

'Of course. I'll be right in.'

'Miss Thomas? I've brought Lane in as chaperon. She's our new HCA. So if you'd like to go behind the curtain and remove everything above the waist and let us know when you're ready...?'

Cole's patient nodded and stepped behind the curtain, pulling it closed behind her. As he waited, he took a moment to re-read the notes from his patient's last few consultations, then he smiled at Lane.

'How are you settling in?'

She still looked a little uncomfortable. First day nerves again?

'I'm all right. Trying to remember how to use the computer system.'

'Have you been away from general practice for a while, then?'

She didn't get to respond as his patient was calling out from behind the curtain. 'I'm ready.'

He indicated that Lane should go first and then he stepped behind the curtain with her, pulling it closed behind them.

Miss Thomas was here because she'd had a double mastectomy and was worried about the healing of her wounds. From what he could see, the left incision was healing nicely, but the right one appeared to be weeping, and it hadn't adhered the way it ought to.

He donned gloves and took a closer look. 'Any pain?'

'A little. But I was told that would be normal anyway.'

He palpated the skin around the wound. It didn't feel hot, but there was still some residual swelling from the procedure.

'I think we ought to take a swab to be on the safe side, and I'll put you on some antibiotics in the meantime— just in case. Lane, could you pass me a swab from over there, please?'

Lane rummaged in a drawer and pulled out what he needed before passing it over.

'This shouldn't hurt, but let me know if it does.'

He gently touched the end of the swab to the weeping wound, trying to make sure he got a good sample to send off to the lab. He capped it off when he was done.

'There you go. You can get dressed now.'

He held back the curtain for Lane to pass through and then closed it again, so that his patient could get dressed in privacy.

'Do you need me for anything else?' Lane asked, not really looking at him, but at some point just over his right shoulder.

Why did he get the feeling Lane was keen to get away from him? *Had* he embarrassed her this morning? Thinking back, he didn't think he'd said anything terrible to her. Perhaps he should take a moment to apologise to her when he could? Because he really didn't want there to be an atmosphere between them. She seemed uncomfortable, and there was something about her discomfort that made him feel he wanted to take it away. People normally felt relaxed and easy-going with him.

Lane had soulful eyes. A deep, mesmerising blue. Almost sorrowful—as if she'd been through a terrible loss. And, having been through a dreadful loss himself, he wanted to make her feel better. Give her a reason to smile.

'If you wouldn't mind taking the swab to the sample collection box in the foyer…?'

It was all he could think of to say. Any other words stuck in his throat. Now was not the right time. He had a patient and they were both professionals.

'And if you could add a note to the patient's file to say that you chaperoned?'

She nodded and took the swab. 'Of course.'

And then she was gone, just as Miss Thomas threw back the curtain and emerged fully clothed once again.

Did the room seem a little dimmer with Lane gone?
How ridiculous! It's probably just the morning light.

Cole smiled at his patient and began tapping at his keyboard to request a prescription for her. He was back in work mode and he'd stay that way until lunch.

Lane dropped the swab into the sample box and took a moment to breathe in the fresh air coming through the open front doors of the practice. That poor woman... A double mastectomy! Had she had preventative surgery? Or had she actually had breast cancer? She'd seemed so young. Her own age. But whatever had happened she was surviving. Perhaps it had been caught early and the doctors had had time to do something about it and save her life?

Lane hadn't expected to be so shocked by it. To be this close to cancer again and stare it in the face. She'd tried to remain impassive in the room, but behind her eyes she'd been fighting back tears, thinking about Skye.

And Dr Branagh had been so nice. Considerate. Interested. And so good with his patient! Not that that should be a surprise, but to see him being so attentive and helpful... Would he have been that way with her best friend? Had Skye made a mistake in not telling him about her pregnancy? Or was this just his work persona?

Lane didn't know. She was used to misjudging men— to having them pull the wool over her eyes and deceive her, making her think one thing when another thing was happening. And it had been agonising to be in close quarters with Cole, knowing that she knew something about him but couldn't tell him. Not yet.

Would there ever be a good time? What was the perfect time to tell a man he was father to an eight-month-old he hadn't even known existed?

And once she told him about Tori he'd want to meet her, surely? Any decent father would. Any decent man would want to do the right thing. And he could make a claim to her in the courts. Skye had never really made it clear whether she wanted Lane to share Tori more officially with Cole, or whether she just wanted her daughter to know her father.

What if he could fight her legally to take Tori away? The thought made her shiver. Goosebumps prickling her skin and she rubbed at her arms to make them disappear.

She headed back inside, knowing she had work to do. She updated Miss Thomas's notes regarding the chaperoning, and then managed to get through an ECG, a double ear syringing, three B12 jabs, two suture removals and a whole host of hypertension checks before lunchtime rolled around.

And suddenly there Cole was again, looking at her weirdly from the kitchen doorway as she nuked her lunch in the microwave. She could feel his intense gaze upon her and she felt unnerved by it.

'Can I help you?'

He frowned, his arms crossed. 'I wonder if I could have a quick word with you? In private?'

He knows! Oh, God, how did he find out?

She swallowed hard and followed him to his consulting room. He closed the door behind her and asked her to sit down in one of the chairs the patients would normally use. She thought he'd sit behind his desk, but he didn't. He grabbed his chair and pulled it out so he could sit across from her, as an equal.

A smile formed upon his face. 'I just want to say that

I hope I didn't embarrass you this morning. It wasn't my intention, and in fact I was very impressed with how you came forward to help.'

Relief flooded through her and the heat she'd felt surging into her cheeks slowly began to drain away. She half laughed. 'Ah, yes… That.'

'I just feel that you're not very comfortable with me, and I don't like that, so if I did anything wrong at all, I apologise.'

Damn it. He's being nice. And respectful.

'No, it wasn't that. It isn't that. No.'

'Then is it first day nerves? I'd like to help if I can. We're all really nice here. We look out for each other and lift each other up—we've always got each other's backs.'

Seriously? Why can't he be an ignorant idiot?

'No, it's not that. It's…'

It's because of who you are. What you did. And how it changed everything. If it hadn't been for you my friend could still be alive, for all I know.

If Skye hadn't met this man, hadn't got pregnant by him, then she might have survived the cancer by having it treated it earlier, instead of continuing with her pregnancy.

'It's nothing. I'm sorry if I made you think that way.'

She tried to sound genuine, look him in the eye, but it was hard. She'd spent months *hating* this man. His very existence, his sleeping with Skye, meant that her best friend's life had been changed for ever—as well as her own. The repercussions had spread out like ripples on a pond. And the way he was looking at her now…

His gaze was intent, and his appraisal made her self-conscious. Those blue eyes of his—so like Tori's—were hypnotic, and they sparkled with a light that she found mesmerising. He was a very attractive man. Short, closely cropped dark brown hair, broad shoulders, and a genuine smile that was warm and inviting.

If she'd been the one to meet him in a pub then she had to reluctantly admit to herself that she would have been enthralled and drawn to him too.

But she couldn't let that happen.

Eventually he nodded, as if he were going to accept her answer for now, even though they both knew it wasn't over.

'Okay. Well, I don't want to keep you from your lunch. We don't get long and I've got a home visit to do.'

It was a relief to be dismissed. 'Right. Okay. Well, I'll see you later this afternoon.'

'What kind of cake do you like?'

She was at the door, her hand on the doorknob, and his question seemed to come from left field. *Cake?*

'I'm sorry?'

'It's my turn to buy cake for everyone, but as you're new I'm happy to get your favourite. What is it?'

She stared back at him, trying to work him out, trying to see if he really was as nice as he seemed to be...

'Lemon drizzle?'

He beamed a smile. 'That's my favourite, too.'

She smiled back at him and felt something lurch in her heart. As if a part of the wall around it was beginning to crumble. The wall she'd so carefully constructed before coming here.

Damn.

She'd only wanted to come here to assess him, tell him the news, and then work out a new 'normal'.

She'd never expected to *like* him.

CHAPTER TWO

THAT WEEKEND LANE decided to take Tori to the bird park just outside Bourton-on-the-Water. Tori loved birds. She especially loved Peter, the macaw parrot that Lane's mother owned, so she was hoping that she'd enjoy the bird park. It would be a welcome outing for both of them. Lane in particular had found her first week at Liberty Point Surgery quite stifling.

Not because of the work. That part was easy. It was because of Dr Branagh and her conflicting emotions surrounding him. She'd spent ages hating a man she'd never met, and now she'd observed him, both with and without patients, and considered him likeable and charming, helpful and kind. And the rest of the surgery staff couldn't sing his praises highly enough! None of it melded with the way she'd thought of him over the last year. She'd pictured a dark, almost mythical figure, cruel and selfish and probably heartless. A man like all the rest—out for what he could get and damn the rest of the world.

Only he didn't seem like that at all. Perhaps he'd never been like that. She was feeling bad for having misjudged him. There were always two sides to a story and she'd never thought to find out his.

'Lane!'

She turned to see who was shouting her name and who should it be but Dr Cole Branagh himself. Looking delightfully casual in a slim-fit checked shirt and jeans? Her heart skipped a beat and she felt her cheeks flush.

'Dr Branagh! What are you doing here?' She skilfully turned Tori's pushchair in the other direction, so that she was facing away from the man who was her father and was instead looking at the flamingos.

'I'm here to support a patient. They're having a Keeper for the Day experience and his parents invited me along.'

Oh. That seemed reasonable.

'That's nice of them,' she said.

'I delivered this boy in the back of a car. He was born with Down syndrome and I've been his doctor ever since. It's his birthday today and he wanted to spend it cleaning out birds. What can I say? The heart wants what it wants.'

She smiled back at him, but her heart was racing and her mind was running through a whirlwind of thoughts and concerns, trying to find a safe topic to talk about and tossing unsuitable ones back into the maelstrom of her mind.

He was less than a metre away from the daughter he didn't know he had. His life could change in a moment. Would he know the second he saw Tori? Would he suspect? Now she knew him a little better, she couldn't help but see him in his daughter.

'The heart wants what it wants.'

Yes. It did.

She swallowed and tried not to blush. 'Well, I won't keep you...'

'You're not! He'll be busy for the next hour or so. They're taking him to the hatchery, so I've got some spare time before they need me back taking photos.' He waved his mobile phone at her and slid it back into his back pocket. 'I didn't know you had a daughter.'

Oh, dear God...

Lane blinked rapidly. 'I don't. She's my...goddaughter.'

She watched in terror as he walked around to the front of the pushchair and knelt down to engage with Tori. She watched him, heart in her mouth, waiting for the axe to fall. Waiting for any tell-tale sign of the horrifying realisation that he was looking at his own daughter.

But it didn't seem to happen. He just smiled at her and waved. 'She's gorgeous. What's her name?'

'Victoria. We call her Tori.'

'Have you given her parents a day off?'

'Something like that.'

This was dangerous territory, and she could almost feel her throat closing up with the fear. He was looking directly at his own daughter! Couldn't he see? Wasn't the magic of blood telling him, screaming at him that he was looking at his own child?

He stood up again, straightened, and she relaxed a little. Keen to get away, she began walking.

'Would you like to grab a coffee?' he asked.

She stopped, tense. 'Oh, I don't know if that's—'

'They do a mean caramel slice in the Jungle Café.'

She hadn't had a caramel slice in years. And if she refused him would it seem weird? They were meant to be trying to be kind to one another. If she backed off again, tried to avoid him, he'd *really* sense something was up and she wasn't ready for that conversation yet. And this way, if she pushed through her discomfort, perhaps she could find out a little more about him? Find out who he really was so she could judge him properly before she dropped her bombshell.

'All right.'

'Great! Let me help you.'

And he reached to take the pushchair handles and began pushing his own baby daughter down the path.

For a moment it was like a glimpse of a possible future. Cole taking Tori out and leaving her behind. She didn't like it. It left her feeling empty and her stomach hurt just at the thought of it.

So with an aching heart, she scurried to catch up, forcing a smile when she got alongside him and trying to get rid of the sense of dread within her heart.

He was right about the caramel slices. They had the perfect amount of rich, buttery pastry and a thick, creamy layer of salted caramel on top that was moreish and went perfectly with their cups of tea. And if it had been any other situation, and any other gorgeous man sitting across from her, she would have enjoyed it. Maybe even flirted a bit if Simon hadn't ruined things so terribly for her.

Instead, she sat opposite Cole, nervous and on edge. Wary of trusting anyone.

'So what made you become a HCA?' he asked her.

'My mum was a nurse and she loved what she did. I used to listen to her tell tales of what had happened at work each day and most of it sounded wonderful.'

He frowned. 'Most of it?'

'She didn't like the long hours. Or how sometimes she'd work past the end of her shift to make sure her patients were okay and then come home to find my dad was disgruntled. He didn't like playing second fiddle to her patients. He left,' she added, realising that she was oversharing. But she did that when she was nervous. She talked. Filled the silences.

'I'm sorry.'

'It's not your fault. And my mum never let the end of her marriage define her. She just does whatever she wants now—without having to ask anyone else's permission.'

She smiled at the memory of her mum doing a sponsored cycle ride to raise awareness of strokes. The day her mum had cooked just short of a hundred cupcakes to raise money for charity. How she still knitted and sewed.

'I grew up wanting to have patients, but without the stress or long hours of nursing. Being an HCA fitted that requirement perfectly.' She leaned forward over the table to turn the focus back on him. To take this opportunity to learn more about Tori's father. 'What about you? What made you become a doctor?'

'Something similar. My mum was a nurse, like yours, and my father was a GP and his father, before him. But it wasn't just because of them, or family tradition. I looked into other career paths, but nothing drew me the way medicine did. It was a calling and I loved every moment.'

Loved. Past tense. She frowned. Curious. 'Loved?' she repeated.

He laughed. 'I still love it. I do. But there have been times when I've felt dreadfully inadequate and useless and I've been angry that I couldn't do more when I needed to.'

He spoke vehemently, and she saw darkness in his eyes as he seemed to look back into his past. Lane knew the feeling well. She'd felt the same, watching Skye slowly die. There were medical advancements being made all the time! Why had none been made in time to help her? Skye had been so bright. So full of life! She'd deserved a long life, but it had been cruelly snatched away by a vicious disease that showed no mercy.

Cole looked sad himself, and she had to fight the urge

to reach out and lay her hand on his. She wanted to. But she still felt that this man was the enemy.

She looked at Tori, happily sitting in the highchair provided by the café, her face smeared with yoghurt.

'We all have those moments,' she said. 'When we wish we could do more.'

He met her gaze and she saw hurt there, and an understanding that she knew all too well. Had she misjudged him? Thinking his life was carefree? That he was a charming Lothario who bedded women left, right and centre, with the only thing to worry about was whether or not he had enough condoms in his wallet?

Ashamed, she broke the eye contact and looked down, grabbing her cup of tea to take a quick sip. It was still hot and burnt her tongue. But she took another sip anyway.

'I'm sorry. I didn't mean to bring up anything difficult.' She pushed the rest of her caramel slice away, having lost her appetite.

'You didn't. I just forget that you don't know.'

Don't know what? She wanted to know, but she also didn't want to push him. Not if it hurt him to bring up memories. He wasn't a charmer of women—he was *human*. He was real. Not the caricature she had made him in her mind before she'd met him. And why would he choose to tell *her* anything? He didn't know her. She was a stranger to him. A new colleague at work.

'My wife died.'

Oh.

'You were married? I didn't know that.'

He smiled and pulled his phone from his pocket, tapped at the screen a few times and brought up a picture of a him and a woman on a ski lift together, laughing and happy in what looked like a blizzard of snow.

'This is the last photo we had taken together before the accident.'

His wife was beautiful. And they looked happy. She quickly glanced at his face and saw love and wistfulness there. He still missed her.

'Where was it taken?'

They were the only words she could squeeze out. She wanted to say, *You look amazing together*, because they did. She wanted to say, *I'm so sorry for your loss*, but it just wouldn't come out, because if it did then she would speak of her own loss and that was too close to home.

'The Alps. We used to go every year, on our wedding anniversary. It was our fourth year there together and we took that ski lift up to the top of a mountain to come down on a Black Run.'

'What's that?'

'It's a ski run for advanced skiers. We'd done it before once or twice, but that day a storm was coming in and we thought we'd make it down one last time before it hit.' He sipped at his own drink, pausing for just a moment as if reliving it. 'We misjudged and the storm caused an avalanche.'

'Oh, my God!'

'We tried to outrun it. To get out of its way. And we were succeeding. Side by side, we raced down that *piste* as fast as we could. But Andrea must have hit something, because the next thing I knew she wasn't there, and I couldn't stop to look for her or I would have been buried alive.'

Lane's mouth felt dry. Her heart was pounding. 'What happened?'

'She was buried by snow. It took three days to find her and dig her out. The worst three days of my life.'

Lane heard raw pain in his voice.

'Her injuries were extensive. Even if we had found her in time she wouldn't have survived.'

'I'm so sorry, Dr Branagh.'

'Cole. Please.'

She gave a single nod in acknowledgement.

'At the autopsy they discovered that she'd been in the early stages of pregnancy. About six weeks. Neither of us had known.'

Lane closed her eyes and instinctively reached out to touch Tori's chubby little hand as she banged her toy down on her tray. To lose not just his wife, but his unborn child...

'I don't know what to say.'

He sighed. 'What *can* you say? These things happen? We should have been more careful?'

She shook her head. 'You weren't to know.'

'I often wonder about that. Whether we should have paid more attention to the weather report. Whether we even should have been up there. It goes around and around in my head all the time. The fact that we took that chance with our lives just so we could have the thrill of conquering a mountain. For the adrenaline rush of showing how good we were? How arrogant is that?'

She shook her head. 'No. You can't blame yourself.'

'Who *do* I blame?'

At that moment Tori began to get agitated, so Lane stood to undo the harness of the highchair and pulled Tori onto her lap, wiping her face with a paper napkin and passing her a beaker of water.

'We all do things we second-guess later.'

He nodded. 'Have you? Did it cost someone their life?'

She flushed and stood, swaying gently with Tori in

her arms. She couldn't tell him about the conversations she'd not had with Skye, because she'd been too afraid to tell her friend to abort the baby she'd so longed for. But should she have been braver? Should she have spoken her mind and told Skye that *her* life was more important?

No. She could never have done it. It had been impossible.

This conversation was becoming too uncomfortable!

Tori dropped her beaker just as a woman was passing by with her children.

She bent to pick it up and handed it to Cole. 'Bless her. She looks just like you. Got her daddy's eyes!' The woman smiled, gave Tori's fingers a little shake and then went on her merry way.

Lane stared at Cole in absolute horror, waiting for the realisation to appear in his eyes, but thankfully it didn't. He simply smiled at the woman as she left and then looked at Lane and laughed. 'They think we're a family. Well, I guess we look like one. A mum. A dad. A baby... What do you think to that Tori, hey?'

Lane wanted out of that café there and then! No hanging around—she needed to go! 'You must be needed back soon? To take photos?'

He glanced at his watch. 'You're right. Thanks for the tea and the chat. It was nice to catch up.'

Nice? It had been the most terrifying thing she'd experienced in months! 'Yes, it was...nice.'

'I'll see you at work on Monday.'

'You will.'

'Would you mind if I took a picture of the three of us? It's a new thing of mine. Trying to record good times. You never know when things could change. And when you're no longer with us, I'll have this memory to remind me.'

When you're no longer with us.

She knew he meant at work. The short contract she had to cover Shelby whilst she was away. But all she could think of was returning to her old life without Tori and that his *with us*, meant him and his daughter. But surely he couldn't do that? He couldn't take her. 'Sure.'

He activated the camera on his phone, came to stand alongside her, then draped his arm around her shoulder as she carried Tori and squeezed her in tight.

Lane looked up at the image on his phone. She could see the way they fitted together—her, Cole and Tori. Like a little family. Just as that woman had thought they were. Tori was smiling, as was he, so she forced a smile too, hoping it reached her eyes and looked genuine.

He pressed the button and saved the image. 'Give me your email address and I'll send you a copy.'

She wrote it on a napkin and handed it over. Then waved him goodbye as he left the café.

She sat there feeling sick and awful. Knowing she had to tell him about his daughter.

He wasn't a Lothario.

He was a widower. And he seemed compassionate and generous and authentic.

'Skye?' she muttered quietly. 'This is too hard.'

He'd not meant to say so much to Lane. She was a work colleague. New. Temporary. But she'd just been so easy to talk to, and it had been nice to sit there with someone—as if they were a little family. Even that woman had thought they were! It had been a long time since he'd been able to sit with someone and enjoy a cup of tea, just chat about life with someone who felt like a friend.

The memory made him smile and he brought up the

picture of them on his phone and looked at it again. He'd been looking at it a lot over the weekend. He knew that woman had only made an offhand comment, but if Andrea hadn't died then he might very well have been sitting there with his own wife and child. Maybe even a daughter, like Tori. The woman had said she'd got his eyes, and now he looked at her image he had to agree. They did look incredibly similar. How odd! Just one of life's strange coincidences...

His gaze went to Lane. She was smiling, but he remembered how tense she had been when he'd draped his arm around her shoulder. Had he overstepped the mark there? He had no idea of her past, he had no idea if she was in a relationship or not, but she certainly seemed uncomfortable with displays of affection.

Or maybe it was just *his* affection? Perhaps she'd felt awkward about it after he'd told her about his dead wife? Or maybe it was nothing to do with that. There could be all manner of reasons why a woman wouldn't want a man to drape his arm around her shoulders. There was so much you had to be aware of as a man, and rightfully so, as far as he was concerned. But he'd done it anyway—without thinking.

Cole, you really need to think about your actions! Isn't that what got you into trouble in the first place?

He put his phone away, then jumped when a red alert box buzzed onto his screen.

Help needed immediately in Reception!

Mary had pressed the alert button. All staff had it on their phone screen, in case they needed help, and it sent out an alarm to every screen in the practice.

He raced from his room and almost bumped into Lane on the way out of hers. He saw the issue immediately. Oscar Jameson was collapsed on the floor of the waiting room.

'Somebody fetch the Resus bag!'

'I'll get it!' Lane replied, turning back to the stock room, where the Resus bag was kept for emergencies such as this.

Mr Jameson was one of his patients. An elderly gent, in his eighties, who lived alone. If he remembered correctly, the medication he was taking included a statin, a blood pressure tablet and some glycerol trinitrate spray for angina.

Cole checked to make sure it was safe to approach the patient and asked the other people in the waiting room to stand back and give them space. He knelt by Mr Jameson and gave him a gentle shake of the shoulders.

'Mr Jameson! Can you open your eyes for me?'

Lane arrived then, with the Resus bag. 'What do you need me to do?'

He knelt to listen for breathing. To watch for the rise and fall of Mr Jameson's chest. Neither happened.

'Get the defibrillator ready. And the bag valve and mask.' He immediately began compressions of Mr Jameson's chest and shouted out an order to Mary. 'Phone for an ambulance!'

Within seconds Lane was cutting away Mr Jameson's clothing to expose his chest. It wasn't hairy, so she was able to place the pads in the correct place quickly. He had no pacemaker. No jewellery to move.

The machine spoke: *'Stop compressions. Analysing heart rhythm.'*

There was a moment of intense silence when Cole had

to fight the urge to *do* something, but he knew he had to wait for the machine to tell him what to do.

'Shock required. Stand clear of the patient.'

Cole made sure everyone was clear of Mr Jameson. 'Shocking.'

He pressed the button on the machine and the shock was delivered. He immediately continued with compressions as Lane smoothly hooked up the bag, valve and mask to the oxygen tank that was carried in the Resus bag. When thirty compressions were up, she performed a head-tilt, chin-lift, and sealed the mask around Mr Jameson's nose and mouth and delivered two breaths before Cole continued.

He was just thinking about which drug to administer when Mr Jameson made a moaning noise and his eyes began to open.

'We've got him. Keep the oxygen on high flow.' He leant down to speak to Mr Jameson. 'You're all right, Oscar. We've got you. You've had a bit of an episode. You're in the doctors' surgery.'

Oscar Jameson nodded and blinked, clearly exhausted by what had just happened.

Cole felt intense relief go through him at getting the man back, but he was very aware that things could still go the other way. He would need to monitor him until the paramedics got there, in case his heart stopped again. He looked at Lane, and her relief was palpable and they smiled at each other. They'd saved this man's life, hopefully.

'You okay?' he asked her, aware that situations like this could be frightening.

She nodded and smiled, her eyes bright with adrenaline. The way she was looking at him right there and then, he might almost have sensed that... No. He was being ridiculous. It was just the heat of the moment, that was all. They were colleagues. Nothing more.

When the paramedics arrived, he handed over the resus details, wishing he could go with them to see his patient all the way through, but knowing there were patients here who still needed him. Especially any that might have witnessed all this and be feeling a bit frightened.

'Maybe I should offer everyone here a drink or something?' asked Lane. 'We have juice in the kitchen.'

He liked it that she was thinking that way. He nodded. 'That would be a nice thing to do. Thanks.'

'And I'll bring you a strong tea. You deserve it.'

'So do you. Thanks, Lane. You were brilliant. I couldn't have asked for more.'

She looked into his eyes and he felt it again. A single moment of such pure attraction that it startled him to his very core. Along with the knowledge that they could be something more if he let it happen. That he could care for this woman if he were brave enough.

But he was afraid. He'd never been in a relationship with anyone since his wife had died. He'd gone out once and got drunk—had slept with a woman who'd run out on him in the morning—but...

Lane wasn't staying here long. She was a stand-in for Shelby who could be back any time. He had no idea how long he would have with her. Best to keep things on a friendship level.

The realisation was a let-down, after the euphoria of saving a man's life, but he had to be realistic. If life had taught him anything, it had taught him that.

When Lane brought him his tea, she set it down on his desk and then sat in the seat that his patients usually sat in.

He looked up at her. 'You okay?'

She nodded hurriedly. Then looked away. As if she felt awkward about something. 'I wonder if we could talk...?'

'Of course! But I have patients waiting right now—and so do you, probably.'

She smiled and nodded again. 'I do. But we need to talk. Sooner rather than later.'

He couldn't imagine what it was about, but clearly she was upset about something. Was it the resuscitation? Did she want to chat through it, make sure she'd done everything okay?

'Okay. Name the place and I'll be there.'

'The bandstand in the park? Say this Saturday, if you're not doing anything? Twelve-ish?'

He nodded. It was a strange place to go to talk, but okay... 'I'll be there.'

She stood up abruptly. Awkwardly. Clearly she was uncomfortable. What was going on that he didn't know about? Perhaps that was what wanted to tell him? He hoped so. He wanted to help.

'I'll see you later, then,' she said. And she went.

He sat there, staring at the door, wondering...

CHAPTER THREE

THE CLOUD COVER was thick as Lane walked towards the park on Saturday. She'd hoped for a better day. A day of sunshine and flowers in which she could drop the news she'd been holding so tightly against her chest and then make a quick getaway.

The last two weeks had proved to her that all her assumptions about Dr Cole Branagh had been wrong. He was a good man. A good doctor. Respected and kind and with a tragic past of his own. He could even have been a father already! But his wife had died and his baby with her. How did you get through something like that and still come out smiling?

Each night she'd gone home and cuddled Tori and played with her, sat with her, read to her at bedtime, and wondered just how much Cole would love to be doing this? How he ought to be doing this and how she was robbing him of precious moments with his child!

But wasn't Tori her child too? Legally anyway. For the last six months Lane had been there—for the first smile, the first laugh, the first tooth…

She was glad she'd made the decision to tell him, because not doing so had started to eat her alive and she couldn't continue that way. Hiding something so monumental. Hiding something that would change Cole's life. The more she kept Tori from him, the more time he lost with his daughter, and she didn't want him to blame her for that. She had always tried to do the right thing. Skye had asked her to decide if he would make a good daddy, and her brain was telling her that he would.

She knew Cole now. Or thought she knew him enough, anyway. He didn't seem the type of man who would take this news lightly and then walk away. He wasn't the Lothario or the charmer she'd imagined. He was just a man. A man she was starting to like. And it hurt to know that she was keeping this secret from him. But parents put their children first, and Tori deserved the right to know her father.

The bandstand was empty when she got there. Clearly the overcast weather was keeping people away from the park. She stood beneath its roof and looked out at the ducks on the pond, noting that on the far side there was a swan. A solitary swan, gliding across the dark surface. She thought about how swans mated for life and wondered where its mate was…

'Good morning.'

Her heart pounded as she heard his voice and she turned to look at him, glad that she'd left Tori with her mother. This conversation could go many ways, and she didn't want to have to worry about what Tori was doing as they talked. She wanted to be present. To explain everything to him.

Would he feel deceived? Would he feel she'd made a fool out of him because she'd arrived in his life under false pretences?

She turned, managed a weak smile. 'Hi…'

He looked good. But he always looked good. He had a

frame that made all clothes look good on him. He could have worn a potato sack and carried it off with panache and style. Was it too late to call this off and just pretend she didn't have to do it?

'How are you?'

'I'm good. A little puzzled as to why I'm here, though, if I'm honest.'

He stood away from her and waited. Unsure.

The bandstand had seats around its edge. She went to one and sat down, looking up at him and telling him with her eyes that he should sit next to her.

He did so, and then he reached out with his hand and covered her fidgeting fingers. 'Whatever it is you have to tell me, it's okay.'

He was comforting *her*. When it should have been the other way around. But she was grateful for his touch and she laid her other hand on top of his. It was trembling. Could he feel that?

'I hope so. I hope you'll understand.'

'Whatever it is, I'm here for you. I know we're colleagues, but I'd like to think we're friends too. We've saved a life, you and me, and that binds us together for ever.'

She smiled at the thought. Mr Jameson was still in hospital, but apparently he was doing very well and was expected to go home on Monday.

'What I have to tell you is…huge. Life-changing, in fact. And I want you to know that I didn't come here to deceive you. I came to…'

She couldn't think of the right words. The words that would be perfect and not hurt him. Because she cared about how he was feeling. He'd been through tough times, too. He'd loved and lost the way she had. And she'd seen how his face had changed, almost imperceptibly when she'd said *deceive*.

She tried to keep back the tears. 'I had to do it. I made a promise.'

'A promise? To whom?'

Soft rain was beginning to fall. She could hear it hitting the roof of the bandstand and she watched as droplets bounced off the leaves of the plants in the flowerbeds close by. She looked out at the park around them, as if it would give her strength to get through the next part. Saw the odd parent scurrying to put up an umbrella or get their kids off the play equipment so they could go home.

'To my best friend Skye. Tori's mother.'

He frowned, clearly not understanding what this was about, or why she felt the need to tell him about it.

She'd practised telling him. She'd stood in front of her bathroom mirror every day this week trying to have this conversation in different variations.

She'd blurt it out—*You're Tori's father!*

She'd say it gently. Angrily.

She'd tried saying it without blame, without expectation, and none of it had seemed right.

How did you tell a man he was the father of a child?

'We grew up together, Skye and I. We met at infants' school and instantly clicked. We had one of those friendships where we could finish each other's sentences, and many people thought that we could be twins.'

He smiled at her, encouraging her to keep going.

His hand was still holding hers. She liked that. His strong fingers were wrapped around her smaller hand. It felt right. Comforting. Supportive. But his being so close, looking at her so intently, was making her heart pound for many different reasons. Some of which she didn't want to examine right now, because nothing would come of her attraction to him. It couldn't possibly.

'She'd been feeling tired for a while. Listless. Lethargic. I'd been telling her to go to the doctor for ages, but she never went. She was scared of doctors. She was an orphan, you see. Had been raised in a care home where every time she saw a doctor he was sticking a needle in her. She said she'd felt like an animal being experimented on. I kept telling her they were only doing their job, but you know how it is... Some people just don't like doctors.'

He nodded. Just listening. Not urging her to hurry in her story. Patient. That was what made him a good doctor. He listened.

'She'd been thinking a lot about who her real parents were. Why they'd given her up. She kept saying the reason she felt ill was because she was a little stressed about tracking them down. Finding out the reason she'd been given away. Then she found her mother, who wanted absolutely nothing to do with her, so Skye went out and got drunk. She ended up going home with a guy but she never wanted to discuss it. Then her sickness got worse.'

'She was pregnant?'

Lane nodded. 'She was shocked at first—but then she was over the moon! She would have someone. A blood relation. Someone who would love her who she was related to. A baby girl or boy she could spoil. But when she went for her scan they discovered the real reason for her sickness.'

'What was it?' Cole's voice was gentle.

'Ovarian cancer.'

She remembered the moment Skye had told her. The way she had broken down into sobs and sunk to the floor.

How Lane had tried to hold her and comfort her, telling her not to worry, that there were things the doctors could do.

Her eyes burned with unshed tears. She looked at Cole through blurry eyes.

'The doctors told her they would try chemotherapy and surgery to treat her, but that her pregnancy complicated matters. The hormones created by the pregnancy were causing rapid growth in the tumour and they were worried that it would spread elsewhere. They told her that if she had a termination they would be able to try to save her life.'

She swallowed. Terrified of the part that came next. The part that angered her the most. She didn't want him to hear the anger in her voice in case he thought she was angry with *him*. This was her own frustration. Her own issue to deal with.

'She refused all treatment so that she could carry her baby to term. She'd never had a blood relative; she wanted her child so much. The doctors warned her not to wait. The cancer had been there for some time. They told her to abort the child. but she refused. I was angry with her for taking such a risk with her life. But I understood why she did it. She knew she wouldn't get to spend much time with her daughter, but she wanted her child to know how much she was loved from the very beginning. That she would never have given her up even for life itself.'

Her turbulent thoughts turned to what had happened afterwards. How much Skye had needed her and how that had torn apart her own relationship with Simon, who'd been so selfish that he hadn't been able to share his own girlfriend!

Cole squeezed her hand tight and brought her back to the present.

'By the time Tori was born, Skye's cancer had progressed so much there was only palliative treatment left. Skye didn't seem to mind. She'd said she'd done the right thing. Her only regret was that she'd never told Tori's father, but she hadn't wanted a stranger to watch her carrying his child while she was effectively dying and feel guilty about it.'

That was one of the things she had loved about her best friend. She had always thought of others first.

Cole's face had changed somewhat. Was he guessing at what she was about to say? Did he know? Did he suspect? Was he afraid of the next words that would come out of her mouth?

'So, Skye tasked me with finding Tori's father and letting him know about his daughter...'

She looked at him hesitantly. Her eyes confirmed what he had to be suspecting.

He let go of her hand and sat back.

Her hand became cool. Wet in the morning rain drifting in on an easterly breeze.

'It's you, Cole. *You're* the father.'

He sat there. Stunned. Lane's words whirling around his head like a storm.

A daughter? How could that be?

But already his brain was convincing him that it was true. There'd been that one night, what would have been his wife's birthday, just after she'd died. He'd not been able to sit alone in their house and he'd gone out to that bar for one drink—which had turned into two or three. Maybe four...

He'd been raging at the world. For its cruelty. Its unkindness. For taking away someone he had loved so much and with whom he'd had so little time. And in the midst of his despair there'd been a woman who had looked just as sad as he had. She'd sat at the bar, her hands wrapped around a whisky glass, staring into its depths, and she'd appeared to have the weight of the world upon her shoulders.

Her pain had drawn him towards her, and he'd asked her if she was okay. The doctor part of him had seen someone in pain and despite his own pain he'd still wanted to help. Her eyes had welled up and his heart had ached for her. And when she'd begun to cry he'd taken her outside for some fresh air. And when they'd got outside they'd begun to talk. And then he'd known the bar was not the safest place for her and had offered to take her home.

'She didn't want to go home,' he said quietly.

Lane looked at him.

'I told her I'd take her home, but she said she didn't want to go. That it wasn't a home—just a house. I didn't intend...' He rubbed at his face, disbelieving, then ran his hands through his hair. 'I took her to my place...got fresh pillows and blankets for the bed. I said I'd sleep downstairs. But somehow we got talking as we sat there, on the edge of the bed, and one thing led to another and...'

He felt his cheeks suffuse with colour as he remembered the guilt he had felt for sleeping with another woman.

'I thought we'd taken precautions, but clearly they didn't work. When I woke she'd gone. I never even knew her name. She left a note, thanking me for looking after her, for keeping her safe and making her feel she was worth something to someone, even if I was a stranger. She signed it with an "S". I guess now I know her name.'

Lane took her phone from her pocket and pulled up a picture of Skye. 'Is this her?'

He took the phone from her, stared at it for a moment. 'Yes. It is. You must think terribly of me. But I didn't take advantage of her, Lane. We were both grieving. I was feeling awful. My wife had been dead for only a few months, it was her birthday and…'

'It's okay. I understand that people deal with things in different ways.'

'I swear I never knew about Tori… I have a *daughter*?'

He suddenly got a flashback to that moment at the bird park, when the woman had said she thought Tori had his eyes, and now he understood the look on Lane's face when that had happened.

So she'd come here to find him? To decide what?

'You're her godmother?' he checked.

'And her legal guardian, as stated in Skye's will. It's all official.'

It was all so much! He was *a father*? To a little girl? 'So she's eight months old?'

Lane nodded, tears dripping down her face. And he knew how fearful she must have been to tell him the truth. He reached up to wipe away her tears and her hand caught at his, as if to stop him.

His breath seemed to catch in his throat. He realised how intimate an act it was and he dropped his hand away fearfully. Did he *really* want to stray into that territory? He'd just had some incredible news broken to him! Did he *really* want to stir the pot even further? He *couldn't* act on his attraction to Lane.

'I'd like to see her. Spend time with her, if I may?'

She nodded. 'Of course.'

'Could I see her today?'

Lane frowned and wiped her eyes. 'Right now?'

'I've already lost eight months. I don't think I want to lose any more.'

CHAPTER FOUR

LANE UNLOCKED HER mum's front door. 'I'm back!'

She could hear Tori chuckling and then there she was, the apple of her eye, being carried in Lane's mother's arms as she came into the hallway.

'This little munchkin has been... Oh, hello. You didn't say we had a guest.'

Cole stood on the doorstep behind her. Lane turned to him, invited him in and closed the door behind him.

'Mum? This is Cole. Tori's father.'

Her mother stared at him for a moment, then nodded. 'Big day for you.' She smiled. 'I best make us all a cup of tea! How do you take yours, Cole?'

'Er...white, please.'

'I'll bring it through. Lane, why don't you take Tori and Cole into the living room?' And she heaved Tori into Lane's arms.

Lane felt the reassuring weight of the little girl and happily nuzzled into her, inhaling her familiar scent and giving her a kiss on one cheek before turning her to face her father.

'Tori? This is your daddy—say hello.'

Tori blew a raspberry and then grabbed hold of Lane's collar and began pulling.

Lane entered the living room and put Tori down on the carpet, near to a box of toys. 'Take a seat,' she said.

Cole seemed to be in another world. As if he were far away and unable to hear. As if he was mesmerised by Tori, watching her.

Lane reached for his hand and squeezed it. 'You okay?'

He seemed to notice her then. Blinked rapidly. 'Yes, I'm fine. It's just…'

'Overwhelming?' She smiled at him to show him that she understood.

'You could say that. Is it okay if I…?' He pointed at the floor and she nodded, looking on as he got down on his hands and knees and sat on the floor next to his daughter. 'Hey, Tori. What's this?' He grabbed a pink brick with a cat painted onto it and tried to get Tori's attention.

Lane watched him for a moment. Had he had any idea when he got up that morning that his world was about to change? To expand? That he would be hit with news so great he would struggle to process his thoughts and understand how he was feeling? That by the end of the day he would have a child? A daughter?

She didn't envy him his turmoil. She knew how she'd felt when Skye had first asked her to be Tori's legal guardian.

She'd always wanted a child of her own, but she'd thought that dream had been put on hold when Simon left her. To be asked to look after Tori had been just what she'd needed to keep her smiling. To give her a reason to get up in the morning and carry on. Especially in the early days after Skye's death, when she had also still been reeling from Simon's desertion. This little girl meant *everything* to Lane.

Suddenly becoming a mother whilst going through the

grieving process had been a huge adjustment. She'd had to adapt quickly, with long days becoming long nights, often with no sleep. There'd been days when she'd just cried, but thankfully on those days, she had been able to turn to her mum for help, and she'd often taken Tori to give her a day to recover—to get her thoughts in order, come back stronger.

And she'd made it. And Tori had become her world. Someone she loved very much and didn't want to have to share. But she would have to if Cole decided to be the kind of father Skye had hoped he would be.

I've done the right thing. I've carried out Skye's last wish.

She watched Cole playing with his daughter. He was doing very well. After all, he was a stranger to Tori, and she could easily have cried and reached out to Lane for reassurance. But she hadn't. Tori seemed to like him, and he was being perfect with her. Letting his daughter decide the game, choose which toys she wanted to play with. Not forcing anything.

His face lit up every time Tori chuckled at him and that made her smile, too.

'Here's that tea, Cole. I'll put it up here on the mantel-piece, where it's safe.'

'Thank you, Mrs Carter.'

'Patricia. Call me Patricia. I'll leave you both to it.'

And then her mum disappeared again, back into the kitchen, understanding that they needed time together to process this.

'She looks like you,' said Lane.

Cole looked up at her and smiled. 'I think so, too.'

'I always thought she had her mummy's smile, but since meeting you I've realised that the rest of her is all her father.' She meant it, and she wanted him to see it. 'You must wish you'd known about her sooner?'

He looked bewildered. 'Well, of course… But life doesn't always work out the way we want it to. I wish Skye had told me. I wish she hadn't run out on me that morning without telling me who she was. I would have liked to make sure she was okay.'

Lane shook her head. 'I asked her about that night so many times. She tried to reassure me that the guy had been very nice. *You* had been very nice. A good listener. She'd been the one who had to listen when the social workers told her that her mother didn't want any contact and she just needed someone to sit and listen to what *she* wanted to say. You gave her that. I couldn't. I wasn't there for her the way I should have been. Perhaps if I had been then all this might never have happened.'

Tori yawned and began rubbing at her eyes.

Lane glanced at the clock. 'It's time for her nap. Let me put her down and then we can talk some more.' She scooped up the little girl, grabbing at her security blanket, about to take her upstairs.

'Wait!' Cole came forward, hesitated, and then planted a small kiss on his daughter's cheek. 'Okay. Sleep well, Tori. You be a good girl.'

Lane smiled and then took Tori upstairs, lying her in her cot, tucking her in and then gently closing the door. Normally she was very good at going to sleep by herself.

Back downstairs, she handed Cole his cup of tea. 'You don't want it to go cold. Mum makes a mean brew.'

He took the cup and sat down on one of the couches.

'How are you feeling?' she asked.

'I don't know! Bewildered, confused. Anxious.'

'I get it. I do. I felt that way, too, when I suddenly had to become a parent.'

'I don't *feel* like a parent.'

'I don't think anyone ever does. I'm assuming you'll want to do a DNA test?'

He smiled ruefully. 'I just need to process this. I think I'm still in shock.'

'You have time.'

Cole nodded. 'I guess we need to sort out what will happen in the future?'

She felt a chill. Already he was thinking about sharing her? How would that work? 'Yes, we do. But that can wait for a while. Get used to the idea, first.'

Cole tried to listen in to the baby's chest, but he kept grabbing at his stethoscope and chuckling. He smiled at the little one and asked his mum if she could hold his arms, but she didn't seem to be able to do it.

'I tell you what—I'll get in my bubble expert.'

He popped next door and rapped his knuckles against Lane's open door.

'Fancy blowing a few bubbles for me? I need to keep a patient occupied whilst I do an exam.'

Lane was wiping down the ECG machine. 'Sure— I'll be right in.'

'Thanks!'

He pulled open his bottom drawer and there was the bottle of bubbles he kept for occasions such as this. Bubbles never failed to entertain and delight, and they were much more interesting than a boring old doctor.

When Lane arrived he passed them to her. 'Little Sam, here, needs to see some of these.'

Lane smiled at him, and the genuine warmth of it,

stirred his insides. She seemed so different at work now. So much more relaxed. Looking back, he could understand how much strain she must have been under, keeping the secret about his daughter, knowing what she was withholding from him.

No wonder she'd seemed stressed and uncomfortable in his presence! And he'd thought it was first-day nerves!

As she blew bubbles, entertaining Sam, he got on with his examination, listening to the baby's chest and checking him over for rashes and high temperature. He seemed fine. He just had a cold, but his mum had been right to bring him in.

He told her it was a virus, and that she could give him infant paracetamol if she thought he needed it, and then said she must bring him straight back if she thought he was getting worse. Other than that, he reassured her, it should pass in a few days.

When Sam and his mother had left, Lane passed him back the bottle. 'Tori loves bubbles, too.'

'Does she?' His heart skipped a beat at learning something new about his daughter. *His daughter.* He had to keep repeating that to himself as it still didn't feel real.

'She does!'

'Then I'll have to buy her some. Could I come round tonight? After work? I'd like to spend some time with her before she goes to bed.'

'I've booked her in to a baby massage class at six, but you could come with us?'

Baby massage? He'd heard lots of good reports about that.

'I'll be there. Shall I pick you up from your house?'

She nodded. 'Know where it is?'

'No.'

She smiled and scribbled her address down on a piece of paper. 'Here you go.'

'I'll look forward to it.'

'Me too.'

She was quite nervous about Cole coming that evening. She wasn't sure why. Maybe because it was the first step, of many, by which he would slowly get to know his daughter more and more. That she had started a process she couldn't back away from now.

And she couldn't stop a small assembly of butterflies from beginning to perform aerial acrobatics in her belly.

Was it because some of the stress had gone? The stress of holding on to the secret that was now in the open? It had been so much easier to talk to each other at work today, and she'd found her thoughts straying to him often. Thoughts that maybe she shouldn't be having... She knew she was attracted to him—even though she'd tried not to be and kept telling herself she *shouldn't* be.

He and Skye had once been together, talking, finding in one another a wounded soul and finding comfort, and that it felt wrong to have the hots for one of Skye's exes.

They'd never gone out with each other's guys—it had been a firm rule, because they'd never wanted anything to jeopardise their friendship. But Skye was gone now, and she'd got to know Cole a bit, and she couldn't stop thinking about him.

But he was Tori's father! And that was all he could be interested in. His daughter. They had a friendship, yes, and it was one she was thankful for. It might easily have been ruined because of the secret, but it hadn't been. He'd not blamed her in any way. Not accused her of tricking him, or taking him for a fool, and she appreciated that.

He'd certainly not given her an ultimatum the way Simon had.

She liked Cole very much.

Maybe that was the problem?

Cole had been nothing but thoughtful, kind and caring. Not to mention handsome and totally unaware of how his looks affected all the women around him. Everyone at the surgery thought he was great. Even Mary the receptionist had a bit of a crush on him—she'd said so. His smile was infectious. And those blue eyes of his, even though they still held a shade of sorrow, could light up in the most beautiful way. They drew you in until you suddenly became aware that you were staring...

Lane liked spending time with him. Getting to know him. She suspected he would be a wonderful father, but she was still going to let him prove that. Because as soon as he did give her irrefutable proof, then what objections could she give?

What if they did get involved? Her and Cole? She wouldn't ever have to share Tori, then, would she? But that was the wrong reason to get involved. Cole had seen how well Tori was connected to Lane. She was Tori's godmother. She had been her mother since she was two months old.

At a quarter to six the doorbell rang and she rushed to answer it. Cole stood there, looking handsome in dark jeans and a white tee shirt that showed the muscles in his upper arms.

Don't look, Lane.

But it was too late. She'd noticed, and her eyes kept stealing glances at him without her even being conscious of it.

'Hi. You made it.'

'Of course. Nothing was going to stop me. Is she ready? Need help getting anything together?'

'No, we're all set. If you could just grab that bag over there? I'll go get the girl of the hour.'

'All right.'

He grabbed the baby bag that she'd filled with soft towels and a bottle of milk for after the session. She'd been told by the massage therapist that a lot of babies got sleepy after a massage, although some got hungry, so it was best to be ready for both eventualities.

She gave him directions and soon they were pulling up outside a house. Janet, the therapist, met them at the door and invited them in, and they were soon in a room full of babies and parents, all sitting on the floor in a circle.

'Right—welcome everyone! You might feel a bit warm! I've increased the heating in this room just a little because we're going to be stripping our babies down. But first, if you could lay the towel that you've brought on the floor for baby to lie on.'

Cole pulled a thick, fluffy towel from the bag, folded it in half and lay it on the floor, smiling across at Lane.

'And when you're ready, let's remove baby's clothes and nappy. Those of you with boy babies might want to have a second towel ready as they tend to like to pee when their bits are exposed to the air.'

There were some chuckles around the room.

'So, let's have the mums go first. Using the grape oil, warming it in your hands first, until they're fully covered, with slow, even strokes we're going to cover their shoulders and chests—like this.' Janet demonstrated on a doll.

Lane watched what she did and began stroking the oil onto Tori's shoulders. It was slippery and smooth but Tori seemed to like it, which was good. She'd never done this before, but she'd wanted to give it a try. Wanted to have as many memories as she could with Tori—they were so important. Like Cole said, you never knew when something might change.

Janet demonstrated how to massage the babies' arms, belly, legs and feet. Cole helped by squirting the grape oil into her hands each time she needed more. He was attentive and seemed to be enjoying himself.

'Okay, let's get the dads to have the babies. Turn them onto their stomachs now.'

Lane and Cole switched places and she watched as he tenderly took his daughter and turned her over onto her stomach. He talked to her all the time, gently whispering, telling her what a good girl she was, how well she was doing.

Janet gave more instructions on how to massage their backs, and again their arms and legs and feet.

Lane noticed that Tori was beginning to drift off. Her eyelids were getting heavy. Cole wrapped her in her towel and lifted her onto his lap, rocking gently as his daughter went to sleep. He looked up at Lane with such happiness in his eyes she couldn't help but smile at his success.

But she felt a little sad, too. And she hated herself for being so selfish.

This wasn't about her, was it? She'd come here to introduce a man to his daughter. To make sure they were good together, to see him be a good father. It had all seemed so simple months ago. But with every passing day the situation became more complicated.

She should be happy that Tori was letting him hold her. Felt comfortable enough to fall asleep in his arms. Lane had done her absolute best at raising Tori, but she had always felt like she was a stand-in and she couldn't help but feel a little left out.

They managed to get Tori in her car seat without her waking and Cole drove them home. He scooped her from the car with those powerful-looking arms of his and gently carried her upstairs and laid her in her crib. He looked down on her with pride.

'She needs Bunny Bee,' Lane whispered, pointing at a yellow bear.

Cole grabbed it and placed it beside his daughter.

'And Tootles.' She inclined her head towards the stuffed black cat that sat in the corner.

He didn't know everything yet, did he? But he would learn. How long would it take? Tori had survived. Lane had survived. So had Cole. They'd all lost someone precious. Now they were connected by that little girl who had got her through a difficult time and brought her immeasurable joy?

'We should let her sleep,' she whispered, and she turned to leave the room, pulling the bedroom door closed gently after Cole.

They both crept downstairs.

'That was amazing, Lane. Thank you for inviting me.'

'It was my pleasure. You need to spend time with each other. Get to know one another.'

He must have sensed the upset in her voice, because he tilted his head and lifted her chin with his finger. 'Hey, I'm not going to steal her away from you.'

She was looking into his eyes then. Those beautiful blue eyes of his. Did he know what kind of effect he was having on her lately? *Did* he? Because if he did then perhaps he wouldn't look at her like that. Or touch her face so delicately.

Those eyes made her want to sink into his arms and lay her head against his chest—have him squeeze her tight whilst he whispered sweet nothings into her ear. The yearning to be held was intense. The desire to feel comforted by him, by someone who would protect her and keep her safe, was something she could easily drown in.

Because for the last few months she'd had to be strong for others. For herself. For Tori. Surely it was someone else's turn to give *her* a soft place to fall?

But, no. She couldn't. Not with him. He was Tori's father and that would be complicated. She wanted to, but wasn't sure if she could.

'I know. It's just… I'm the one who's looked after her all this time. I love her like she's my own.'

'She's a very lucky little girl to have you.'

'She should have been luckier. She should have had her *real* mother.'

He nodded. 'Did Skye get to see her? Hold her? When exactly did she die?'

Lane sighed heavily. 'Tori was two months old when her mother passed away.'

'You've looked after her since then?'

'Since she was born, really. Skye was so sick towards the end and she needed me to care for Tori. The cancer had metastasised to her bones, her liver, her brain, her lymphatic system… She gave birth a month early. The doctors insisted upon it. They said the pregnancy was an added strain to her body.'

Cole nodded. 'I wish I'd known.'

His tone was so heartfelt she had no doubt that he was telling the truth. But this was getting awkward now. Standing at the bottom of the stairs, talking about Skye's death. It reminded her of Simon, too. His ultimatum. Him, or Skye and the baby? She wasn't used to a man being kind to her. She really needed him to go now, so she could clear her head.

'Do you want a coffee?' The words were out before she realised she'd said them.

'I'd love one. Thanks.'

He'd not expected the evening to go so well. He'd thought only Lane would get to do the massaging and he would watch as some weird spectator, feeling like a spare part when all he wanted to be was be *involved*. Doing something. Being part of this little girl's life now that he knew about her. He'd already missed so much! He didn't want to miss anything more.

Yes, it had been a shock. And he felt bad that Skye had not felt able to tell him the reason she'd been in that bar, staring into her glass with tears in her eyes. He'd always thought he was an approachable guy, someone people could talk to. It was part of why he felt he was such a good doctor—people felt able to confide in him.

But because he'd still been in the depths of a depression himself that night he hadn't pushed enough. Had just listened when she'd spoken about how alone she felt. How she had no one. He'd sensed depression in her. Had recognised a kindred spirit, currently suffering, and for a brief while they had given each other comfort in the only way they could.

It had never been about having crazy sex with a stranger. It hadn't even been about celebrating still being alive. It had been about two lonely people, needing to find comfort in the arms of each other. As simple as that. And it *had* given him comfort for a while—though afterwards he'd lain in bed and felt guilty that on his wife's birthday he'd taken another woman to bed. He'd hoped that Andrea would have understood. That she wouldn't have minded that he had sought solace from someone else who was hurting and that for a brief time they had made each other's world just a tiny bit brighter.

And yet somehow he now had this beautiful little girl in his life, and a second chance to do everything right.

Little Tori had let him massage her without crying. She had let him hold her until she went to sleep, and he had settled her into her crib for the night. He'd wanted to stoop down and press a kiss upon her cheek, but he'd been distracted by Lane telling him which cuddly toys his daughter liked to sleep with and suddenly absorbed in soaking that information in.

He would need to know this. He would need to know so much more! And he couldn't think of anyone better to learn from, than Lane.

Tori knew this woman as if she were her mother. And that was why he understood the look in her eyes when they'd stood at the bottom of the stairs and her face had looked a little sad.

It was clear the two of them had a great relationship. Not once had he heard Tori cry. She seemed a happy baby and that was thanks to the care and love that Lane had provided. There was no way he was going to just dismiss that.

Cole accepted the mug of coffee she pressed into his hands and waited for her to sit down on the couch opposite.

Her place was nice. Warm and comforting. He noticed a couple of pictures of Skye on the mantelpiece. Did she have others? And there was a huge bookcase, filled with fiction, that he longed to go to and look at to see what kind of books she liked to read.

'I want you to know I appreciate how difficult this must be for you,' he said.

Lane looked across at him. 'Do you?'

'I do. I know how I'd feel if I was in your position.'

She smiled. 'Well, I *was* in your position, once. Suddenly having a daughter after going through a great loss. It's a lot to take in.'

'It certainly is. And I want you to know... I guess what I really want to say is that you can count on me. I'm not going to walk away. I'm here. I can be depended upon. You can trust me.'

She looked down at the ground, then back up again. Clearly she was thinking about things that she didn't want to say. Was she afraid to say them?

'I'd like to stay involved in Tori's life—if you'd like me to, of course.'

He'd meant to show that he was open to how this relationship was going to go. That he didn't want to stand on Lane's toes, or demand anything.

This was so difficult. Of course he was going to make mistakes here! But he didn't want to upset Lane. Or Tori. Not at all. And the realisation of that made him realise just how much he cared for the both of them already.

'You're clearly the most important person in her life. You're her godmother. You'll never lose her. She will always know who you are and how important you are.'

He hoped that sounded better. Her face seemed to soften. It gave him hope that he hadn't offended her too much.

'She's my world, Cole. My reason to keep going. These last few months it's been hanging over my head, knowing I had to find you. In the early days I was still struggling to cope with my grief and raise a baby. I knew time was ticking away. Counting down. I never wanted to knock on your door and just tell you what had happened. I didn't think you'd believe me. I had no idea what kind of man you were. So, once I was properly on my feet, and knew what I was doing, I got the job at the surgery to see. Part of me hoped I could walk away without ever telling you, so I didn't have to share her. But now you know, and it *terrifies* me, because she has been all I've thought about for what seems like a lifetime. I could never let anyone hurt her.'

He understood that. 'Then we need to find a way to make this work for both of us. And for Tori.'

'Yes. We do.'

'A routine. A structure. So we don't confuse Tori, either.'

'All right. What do you suggest?'

He thought for a moment. 'Maybe to start with I could come round each evening? To play with her? Maybe take her for a walk? Get her ready for bed and put her down?'

'Okay. And what about weekends?'

'I can do whatever fits in with you.' He needed to show her that he wanted to work with her on this. He didn't want to seem like he thought he was the one who got to call the shots. She was the guardian, not him.

'I like to take her out at weekends. There's a Faery Fayre this Saturday. Everyone gets to dress as fairies. So you probably wouldn't want to do that.' She smiled.

He grinned. 'Are you kidding? I'd love it.'

'Really?' She looked surprised.

'Absolutely. Tell me when and where and I'll be there.'

Lane laughed out loud when she saw him at her door on Saturday morning. He wore his usual jeans and a shirt, but he also wore a large pair of fairy wings attached to his back and he had a swirl of green and pink glitter running along his cheekbone and curved around his left eye. He even held a silver wand.

'What do you think? Will I blend in?' He smiled at her.

Lane couldn't stop laughing. He looked like a *dad*. A dad trying to please his daughter. 'I think you might! Come on in. Come see my own little fairy.'

She led him through to the living room, where Tori sat on the floor, pink wings attached to her back by the elastic straps around her arms. She squealed and waved her arms when he appeared.

Cole stooped down to pick her up and settled her on one hip. 'You look beautiful! But, then again, you're beautiful anyway. Ready to rock the fairy world?'

Tori blew a raspberry and a bubble escaped her mouth.

'I'll take that as a yes,' he said. He turned to Lane. 'Anything I can help with? I've packed a small picnic basket in the car.'

'Oh! Right… That's great. Thank you. I just need to grab my wings and then we can go. Shall we go in my car? It means not having to keep moving the car seat.'

'Perfect. I'll grab the picnic from mine.'

They got Tori settled in her seat, after removing her wings, then Cole removed his so he could put on his seatbelt. When the engine started the usual music began. A woman's voice singing about the wheels on a bus.

Cole began joining in with the song and Lane smiled as she drove them to the fayre. How had she suspected he would be a terrible dad? He was giving this one hundred percent! Most men would shun the idea of dressing as a fairy, but not him! He'd gone for it—including make-up!

She reminded herself to take a photo of him when they got there.

Parking for the fayre was busy. She hadn't realised how busy it would be, and they had to park in a faraway field and put their wings back on before making their way back to the village high street, where the main fayre was being held.

There were flowerpot shies, instead of coconut shies. Stalls selling fairy outfits. A face painter. A bouncy castle. Lots of stalls selling food. There was even a dog show, with the dogs dressed as fairies! The cutest one Lane saw was a tiny little pug puppy, with purple wings and a small tiara on its head. And most people had made the effort too. Everyone was smiling—it really was perfect.

Cole bought them both some pink candy floss, and then he bought her a beautiful lei of pink and yellow flowers that he draped around her neck. She was having so much fun! She might almost believe they were a family.

She forced the thought out of her mind and pulled her phone from her pocket. 'Let's take a picture.'

Cole leaned in and she snapped the shot, showing it to him.

He grinned. 'Let's take one with Tori near all those balloons.'

He unclipped her from her pushchair and went over to a balloon seller, who had helium balloons of all designs—unicorns, rabbits, foxes, ladybirds. Just as she took the photo Tori turned to look at her father and laughed. It was a perfect moment. One that warmed her heart and made her want to be in the picture with the two of them.

'Excuse me,' she asked a woman passing by with her own children. 'Could you get a snap of us all together?'

The woman nodded, smiling, and Lane posed with Cole and Tori.

'What a great dad!' the woman said as she handed back the phone. 'My hubby refused to come!'

That made Lane feel good. Some men wouldn't feel comfortable coming to a fairy fair and dressing in wings and make-up, but Cole did. He was proving to her that he would go the extra mile to make memories they could look back on and smile. He was selfless and she was enjoying his company.

Why had she ever thought she was in love with Simon? The man had been the definition of selfish!

'Thank you.' She slipped her phone back into her pocket. 'Ooh, look—a fortune-teller! Shall we see what she says?'

Cole laughed. 'If you like. Do you believe in that sort of thing?'

'Not really, but I think it will be fun.'

Lane led them over to the small marquee where the fortune-teller sat. Her name was Melrose, and on her table she had a crystal ball, as well as a deck of tarot cards, and a sign told them she read palms, cards and minds!

Melrose invited her to sit down and Lane held out her hand for her palm to be read.

The fortune-teller gazed at her hand for a moment. 'You have a long, clear life line here.'

Lane smiled. 'Does that mean I'll live a long time?'

Melrose neither admitted it nor denied it. 'Your love line is straight, but then—do you see this curve here—it seems to take off? That's because you've found true love.'

'Okay...'

Found true love? Melrose was saying she'd already found it? Well, she had to be wrong, didn't she, because she was single right now. And she couldn't be referring to Simon, because there was no way *he* was her true love!

She glanced nervously at Cole, who held Tori in his arms. It couldn't be Cole. Yes, she liked him a lot—and, yes, she was attracted to him, but… No, fortune-telling was just a bit of fun, that was all. Nothing scientific about it. Nothing *real*.

'Your marriage line, here, is whole. Uninterrupted. Your relationship will last.' Melrose looked at both Lane and Cole.

The fortune-teller thought they were married!

'Oh, we're not together!' Lane explained, cheeks flushing furiously. 'We're colleagues, but nothing more!'

Melrose smiled and leaned back. 'You have some surprises coming your way.'

'What kind?'

'You'll travel overseas together.'

Overseas? Like…to a medical conference? Lane didn't think this fortune-teller was very good at all—but then again, what had she expected?

'And there will come a moment, quite soon, when you will have to make a leap of faith.'

'In regard to what?'

'That's all your palm shows. It's impossible to give exact details.'

Lane walked away from the fortune-teller feeling slightly aggrieved. She'd known it would just be a bit of a laugh, but for some reason she'd hoped—just a tiny bit—that the fortune-teller would tell her something that would ring true. In fact, she'd got almost everything wrong, and guessed at things in the future that were very vague.

She'd been the worst of cold readers and it was something that Lane would never try again. And what about the leap of faith. Had that already happened? When she'd chosen Skye and the baby over Simon? It had to be that.

It couldn't possibly be anything else.

Cole hadn't expected to feel hurt when he heard Lane explain that they were colleagues and nothing more. He'd thought they were more than that. More than people who just worked together. He'd hoped that they were at least friends.

She was the legal guardian of his daughter. He was the father. Yes, they worked together—temporarily—but he was making a real effort to make Lane feel that she belonged both at work and in this relationship they were forging. Yes, it was a work in progress, and perhaps it always would be, but to say they were nothing more than *colleagues*…? That suggested a distance between them. A distance that he'd hoped wasn't there.

Perhaps he was reading too much into what was happening here? Perhaps he ought to be focused on being the best father he could to baby Tori? Because *she* was the important one here and *she* was the one he didn't want to lose.

I don't want to lose Lane either.

It was perfect right now, wasn't it? The three of them. He was the father and she, technically, was the mother. They were a perfect little family.

Why would he want to change anything? But maybe he had to clarify his thinking? Be the best father Tori needed, be a good colleague to Lane and leave it at that? After all, did he really need to be involving another woman in his life? And his building feelings towards Lane were making him feel guilty. What if all this ended in a bad way? After all, it was what he was used to happening…

But even as he tried to convince himself that he needed to make a clear boundary with Lane a small voice in his head was shouting that it wasn't what he really wanted. That what he wanted was to be close to Lane. He looked at her now, pushing the buggy in her fairy wings, her dark brown hair swinging as she walked. He looked at the set of her jaw, the shape of her full mouth. The way she was biting that bottom lip as if she were thinking about something…

He had to look away. Concentrate on where he was going. There were so many people here!

Tori began rubbing at her eyes. Was she tired?

'Let's put this one in her buggy,' said Lane. 'I think she may go to sleep.'

He gently laid Tori in her seat and strapped her in safely, then gave her the cuddly toy she liked to hold when she slept.

Look at us. The three of us.

This could have been the family he'd once dreamed of doing stuff like this with. Here it was—his chance to enjoy it to the full—and all he could think of was that Lane had said they were colleagues and nothing more.

'You all right? You look…odd.'

She'd noticed. 'I'm fine,' he said.

'Maybe I should sprinkle some fairy dust on you? To make you look magical again, like you did this morning.'

He smiled at her attempt to cheer him up. She wanted them to be on good terms and so did he.

'Fairy dust?'

She pulled a small pouch from her pocket. It was filled with glitter. 'I bought some at a stall. You never know when it might come in handy.'

'It's glitter.'

'It's *magical* glitter. And it's environmentally friendly. Come on—hold out your hand and make a wish.'

He didn't want to. He felt silly. But, then again, he was standing there wearing fairy wings, and he had glitter on his face already, so what were a few more sparkles?

He held out his hand and she poured some glitter into it.

'Now, squeeze your hand tight, make a wish and then scatter it over your shoulder. Just make sure no one's walking behind you when you do—we don't want to blind anyone.' She laughed.

He liked the way her smile and her laughter lit up her face. It did something wonderful to her eyes. They *gleamed*. She was having a good time, and he didn't want to spoil that. So he squeezed his hand tight.

What to wish for?

To get to know Tori more? Or for a more formal arrangement with her? He looked into Lane's smiling face and the thought came unbidden.

I wish I could kiss Lane.

His gaze went to her smiling mouth. Her lips...

What? Where did *that* come from? He felt his cheeks colour and he scrambled to think of Tori instead as he threw the glitter over his shoulder.

'What did you wish for?' asked Lane.

'I can't tell you. Then it won't come true!'

She laughed and squeezed her own hand and her eyes tight shut.

He stared at her, welcoming this moment to just look at her and not have her observe him. Her childlike glee was mesmerising. What was *she* wishing for?

You could take this moment and kiss her.

He shook his head, trying to clear the thought. He couldn't kiss Lane. She was Tori's guardian. Her godmother. His *colleague*. If he did it would complicate all that was going on with them already—and they had enough between them to deal with without a romance, too.

What if they got together and the relationship didn't work out? How would that work with Tori? It could be a bitter split and she could take away his daughter. He didn't think she would—she seemed a nice person, and not the vindictive kind—but what if it happened? He couldn't lose Tori now and know it was his own fault. He'd lost his wife through a stupid mistake—he wasn't going to mess this up, too.

Lane opened her eyes and threw the glitter over her shoulder. 'Wish made. Let's hope they both come true.'

He smiled at her and nodded. 'Let's hope.'

CHAPTER FIVE

THEY WERE WALKING ALONG, thinking about where to have their picnic, when they noticed a small crowd of people up ahead. Lane looked at Cole, who frowned. It looked as if there was someone on the ground.

'I'll take a look.'

Cole dashed forward, gently pushing his way through the gathering.

Lane watched him get swallowed up by the crowd and thought she glimpsed blood on the person, but couldn't be sure.

Then she heard, 'Has anyone got any bandages?'

Her heart began to pound. Clearly someone was in trouble! She wanted to help too. Cole might need her.

She began to push her way through the crowd, using the buggy like a snow plough. 'Excuse me! I can help!'

The crowd parted and let her through and there, reminiscent of her first meeting with Cole, she saw an elderly lady lying on the ground. But this time she saw, beneath the woman's right leg, a lot of blood soaking into the grass.

'Cole?'

'Somebody call for an ambulance, please,' he said calmly. 'Let them know there's a doctor on scene, but tell them they need to get here as soon as possible with a pressure bandage.'

His hands clasped the lady's leg and they were slippery with blood. An elderly gent—the woman's husband?—passed Cole a white handkerchief, clean and pressed into a square, from his pocket.

'It was an accident, Doctor. I didn't mean to do it!'

'What happened?'

'I was walking behind her with the trolley, in case she needed to sit down. Her legs haven't been too good lately. There was a bump in the grass and I pushed too hard to get over it—the trolley went into the back of her leg.'

Lane could see that the lady had frail, friable skin. It must have been ripped open by the metal of the trolley.

Cole had the handkerchief pressed tightly against the wound, but blood was coming through. They would need a pressure bandage quickly if she wasn't to lose too much.

'What's your name?' Cole asked the lady.

'Freda. Freda Mallard. Like the duck.'

Cole smiled. 'Well, you're bleeding, Freda, so I'm going to keep my hand tight here to try and stop it—okay? Are you on any blood thinners?'

'Warfarin.'

Lane's heart sank slightly. Warfarin meant her blood wouldn't clot as fast as normal and she could potentially lose more volume. If she fainted or went into shock...

This was hardly the best place for this sort of thing to happen.

Lane knelt beside her, one hand clutching Tori's buggy, the other reaching out for Freda's hand. 'I'm Lane. I work with Dr Branagh, here, and we're going to look after you—all right? Tell me about yourself and your husband. When did you meet?'

It was important to try and make Freda focus on other matters than her leg. If she was right, this elderly lady would have a bit of the Blighty spirit and not panic.

'At a dance. He took my hand when Elvis came on and we jitterbugged to one of his songs.'

'A jitterbug? You must have had loads of energy.' Lane smiled.

'Well, in those days we did. Not so much now.'

Lane could hear sirens in the distance and began to relax slightly. Freda looked pale, but not too bad. And of course she had no way of knowing if this was Freda's natural colouring.

'Do you hear that, Freda?' Cole asked. 'Help is on its way.'

'Help is already *here*,' Freda insisted. 'I've got a fairy doctor, of all things! What do you think you've been doing?'

He smiled. 'I mean proper help. With the right equipment. The only thing I've got on me is fairy dust.'

'Well, a sprinkle of magic might help, Doctor—you never know!' Freda chuckled.

'Once we've got you in that ambulance I'll make a wish for you. To have a speedy recovery.'

'All right.' Freda smiled at him, clearly comforted by his good nature. 'Maybe just wash those hands of yours first, eh?'

Cole laughed. 'Definitely.'

'Will you come and visit me? It's been a long time since a young man held my leg so wonderfully, and I'm not sure I can let you go.' She chuckled as her husband clicked his tongue.

'She always was a flirt, Doctor. Watch your husband, young lady, before she makes off with him!'

Again people thought they were together! She made eye contact with Cole and smiled at him, but he looked away and her smile dropped. Had he not heard? Or did the thought of the two of them being together upset him that much? Yes, he was a recent widower, but she'd thought that they were getting along. Perhaps he still felt loyal to the memory of his wife? She couldn't possibly compete with the woman who'd once been the love of his life. Or perhaps he was just pretending to like her so he could get her onside? Men had always used her, or let her down, and right now Cole had it made—a daughter with a ready-made mother.

The thought chilled her, and she let go of Freda's hand so she could get out of the way as the paramedics arrived with their overstuffed green bags and began to get their equipment ready.

She stood holding Tori's buggy—thankfully she'd slept through the whole thing—and watched as Cole gave his analysis of what had happened to the paramedics.

He was good—she had to give him that. Calm. Collected. And he built a rapport with his patients immediately. Had even done so with her.

But to what end?

What was his endgame? To try and claim his rights as a father? To go to court? To fight her for custody? Was that possible? She didn't know. Had all she'd done—all the sacrifice, all the upset—been for nothing? What rights did she have?

I don't actually know. I should!

Would he give her an ultimatum one day? The way Simon had?

Give me my daughter or...

A bystander gave Cole a bottle of water to rinse his

hands with, and once the blood was gone he wiped them dry on his trousers.

'I'm just going to see Freda into the ambulance,' he told her.

She smiled and nodded, watching as he walked behind the paramedics, fairy wings glinting in the sunshine, with Freda in a chair and Freda's husband walking by his wife's side.

Look at him. So caring. So dedicated! I'm being awful, doubting him in this way.

What had he actually done to make her think so badly of him? Nothing! Absolutely nothing! He'd just given her a look that she might or might not have misread. That was all. If anything, this overreaction of hers was Simon's fault—for making her feel this way about anyone who seemed to want to get to know her. For always thinking that men were only out for themselves.

Lane had quiet words with herself as she waited with Tori for Cole to get out of the ambulance once he'd helped Freda's husband in and made sure he was seated safely in the back. He closed the door and waved through the blacked-out window, knowing that those inside could see him even if he couldn't see them.

He's a good man. He's given me no reason to doubt him.

Yes, he was a *very* good man, and his wife had been lucky to have him. He clearly cared deeply.

She wondered how long it would be before a guy like Cole cared about her the way she wanted to be cared for. She wanted to be loved intently. Genuinely? But how would she ever trust anyone to let them try?

The words of the fortune-teller came back to her— *'You've found true love.'*

Had she? Where? Perhaps she'd already lost it?

Or was it Cole?

Everyone they met seemed to think they were a family already—and maybe they were in their own little way. It was a different kind of family, but did it make them any less than any other? It was just a bit broken. In pieces. Maybe they were like a patchwork? Separate pieces being sewn together? And wouldn't that be perfect? The three of them together?

Perhaps Cole would take her overseas, like the fortune-teller had said. Maybe a trip somewhere with Tori—something like that.

Because surely it couldn't be anything else?

What was real?

And what was just fantasy and fake fairy glitter?

CHAPTER SIX

'YOU'VE BEEN QUIET the last few days. Are you all right?'
Cole had noticed a change in Lane since the Faery Fayre.
She was still her usual smiley self with patients and their
colleagues at the surgery, but at other times, in quieter
moments, he'd noticed that she seemed quite subdued.

'I'm fine,' she answered, nodding her head, before
turning back to vacantly waft through the pages of a magazine during their lunch break.

He wasn't sure he believed her. But he didn't want to
say so outright. 'Everything all right with Tori?'

Again the nod. 'Fine!'

Waft. Waft. Waft.

He tried to think of what this could be about. Not the
fayre That had been a *good* day—medical emergency
included! He'd checked up on Freda and discovered that
she'd been bandaged up and returned home. He'd thought
he and Tori had had a good day out—even if one or two
people had thought they were a family!

It had been bittersweet each time that had happened.
He'd wanted to be part of a family for so long! To be a
good father. A good husband. He'd failed the last woman
he'd promised his life to. He'd not kept her safe. He'd not
immediately noticed when she'd fallen behind, and when

he had it had been impossible for him to stop and go back. The first rule of attending any medical emergency was to check that it was safe to approach, and with the blizzard and the avalanche he would have died himself by going back.

Perhaps he ought to have gone? If he'd loved Andrea as much as he thought he had, then surely...

No. Stop it. You've been through this. It wasn't your fault. You did what you could.

He looked at Lane. She was telling him she was fine but clearly she wasn't, and perhaps this was the moment for him to make sure she was all right in every way? To go back and check? Because fate had taught him one thing so far: that a happy future was not guaranteed.

She'd been through a lot in the last year, hadn't she? Losing her best friend to cancer. Taking on a daughter. Fulfilling the wish of a dying woman to seek him out and share the baby she had come to love.

But sharing meant sharing with him. Perhaps she didn't want another man in her life. 'I understand this is difficult for you.'

She stopped wafting, looked straight ahead. 'What?'

'Tori. She knows you. You're her world. I appreciate that by being her mother you also have to put up with me. And you never asked for that.'

She glanced at him.

'Tori trusts you. Loves you. One day, I'd like her to feel the same way about me.'

Lane put down the magazine. 'Of course I want you to have that.'

He wanted to reach out. Lay his hand upon hers to emphasise that her friendship meant the world to him. But he couldn't. Because he knew that if he did, he'd want to do more. He'd want to move closer to her. To squeeze her hand tight and look deep into her eyes until she smiled at him. And then he would lose himself in that smile, and he wasn't sure if he was ready, if he was brave enough, to lose himself like that again.

Instead he managed a brisk smile, because that was safer, and because with the adrenaline rushing through his body he couldn't just sit there and—

'It's my birthday this weekend,' she said.

He turned. 'Is it? I didn't know that.'

'Skye and I would always go to the seaside on my birthday. We'd walk down the pier and play amusement arcade games, eat fish and chips and come home with armfuls of the cuddly toys we'd won on those silly grabby machines.'

She looked wistful, and he realised this would be the first birthday she'd spend without her best friend. That must be why she'd been so subdued lately. Birthdays and anniversaries after the death of a close loved one were always hard. He knew that.

'I'm sorry she's not here to do those things with you.'

'I knew it was coming, though. I've been trying not to think about it and telling myself it doesn't matter, but… It'll be strange not to go.'

'I'll take you,' he blurted out, and then he felt hot. Because he hadn't realised those words were going to come out of his mouth, and now that they were out, he couldn't go back on them.

Of course it would be fun to spend the day with Lane— he couldn't think of anything better—but the more time he spent with her, the more he wanted to touch her and hold her in a way that went far beyond them being just colleagues.

'You can say no,' he said.

But he'd seen her eyes light up at the idea, at the *hope* of going. 'You'd really take me?'

'I can't think of a better way to spend the weekend. We could take Tori.'

She grimaced. 'My mum's taking her for the day, to go and visit my aunt and uncle in Cirencester. She wanted to give me the day off. It was arranged ages ago.'

All that time alone. Just him and Lane. Without the distraction of Tori. The *chaperonage* of Tori.

'Oh, right…'

She looked disappointed. 'You only wanted to go if Tori was with us, didn't you? Of course. I should have realised—'

'I'd love to take you to the seaside.'

She stared at him as if trying to read him. To see if he was telling the truth. 'Are you sure?'

No, he wasn't sure. He'd never thought he'd feel attracted to another woman the way he'd felt attracted to Lane—not after his wife died—but here he was! Agreeing to a day-long date.

But how hard can it be? I've got self-control, and Lane doesn't see us as anything but colleagues, so…

'I'm absolutely sure.'

He smiled and nodded.

Just to prove it.

Lane had butterflies in her belly when she heard the doorbell, wondering how she was going to get through a whole day with Cole, without the distraction of Tori, and also how it might feel to be at the beach without Skye for the first time in years.

But when she answered the door she burst into laughter, because Cole stood there holding a massive bunch of helium balloons that he had to fight through, just to see her face.

'Good morning! Happy birthday!'

He thrust the balloons towards her, and she was smiling so much her cheeks hurt.

Just moments before she'd been crying, because her mother had given her a birthday card that Skye had written before she'd died. It had been unexpected, and it had reopened the door to all the grief she'd been stamping down on over the last few months.

'Let me put these somewhere.' She took them through into the living room and placed them in the corner by the window.

When she turned to face him her heart stuttered. He looked gorgeous today, dressed in dark jeans and a slim-fit black shirt that showed off his trim waist and broad shoulders perfectly. But that wasn't her main focus. Her main focus was his smile.

'And I got you this.' He passed over a small gift bag.

'Oh, you didn't have to get me anything.'

'Are you kidding me? Of course I did. We're…friends.'

Friends. She noted he hadn't said *family.* But then again, they weren't family, were they? She was Tori's guardian, her godmother, but the two of them weren't blood-related, like Tori and Cole were. They were father and daughter. Lane was an outsider to that. No matter what the paperwork said, he and Tori would be closer in some ways than she could ever be.

'Should I open it now?'

He nodded.

She opened the bag and reached in, pulling out a small square box. Jewellery? With shaking hands she slowly opened it, and gasped in surprise.

Inside was a beautiful silver bracelet with three charms on it. One charm was the letter S, the second, the letter T, and the third charm the letter L. *Skye. Tori. Lane.* Her beautiful goddaughter sandwiched between her and her real mother.

'This is beautiful!'

'You like it? I wasn't sure what to get you.'

'I love it.'

She went to put it on, but couldn't do it with one hand, so Cole came forward to do it for her. She stood there, heart pounding with Cole so close to her, breathing in his scent and his nearness, watching the way his fingers so deftly and easily fastened the bracelet around her wrist.

'Thank you. But where's your initial?'

He smiled. 'It seemed a bit presumptuous to put that on there.'

'You're Tori's father!'

'Yes, but the bracelet is about the special relationship the three of you had. What you forged together. I'm not a part of that.'

She looked up at him with awe and wonder at his thoughtfulness, and she just wanted to kiss him right there and then. Then she realised what she'd just thought of doing and felt her cheeks flush with heat.

'Well, I'm going to get the letter C put on as soon as I can.'

'Isn't it bad luck to buy charms for your own bracelet?'

She laughed. 'I don't believe in that nonsense. Besides, the worst things in life have already happened, haven't they? And we didn't buy any charms for our own bracelets before any of those happened.'

He laughed. 'I guess not. So, are you ready to get

going? We've got a long drive if we want to get to Weston before lunch.'

'Let me just grab my bag and we can go.'

She looked at him then. Truly looked at him. He was giving her everything. Reassuring her. Treating her right. He was so kind, and she doubted she would ever meet another man like him.

'Thank you, Cole. I mean it.' And she reached up on tiptoe to kiss him on the cheek.

Her lips brushed his skin, feather-light, but enough to feel the hint of bristles on his jaw and to feel her own skin against his. It was the briefest of moments but it would be etched into her memory for ever.

'It was my pleasure,' he said, his voice rough.

He was thankful to be driving. It gave him something to think about other than that kiss she'd given him.

Oh, who am I kidding? It's all I can think about!

He'd wanted to get her a gift she could treasure, but when he'd thought about what to get he'd realised he knew almost nothing about her! Apart from Tori, what else had they talked about? Skye, obviously. His wife, Andrea. But had they ever talked about Lane?

He didn't know her favourite anything. He didn't know what she'd been like when she was at school, if she'd ever had anyone special, what she'd wanted from life before cancer had taken Skye and given her Tori and changed the direction of her life for ever.

All he really knew was how special their relationship had been, so he'd got her something that would commemorate that for ever.

And she'd kissed him.

It had been a quick peck on the cheek, but when she'd

leaned in the way she had, on tiptoe, pressing one hand to his chest, he'd wondered if she'd felt his heartbeat quicken, if she'd noticed the longing in his eyes and the disappointment that he'd felt when she'd drawn away.

And then the guilt had set in. Of course it had! It was his constant companion.

It had plagued him for ages, keeping him solitary, keeping him alone. He'd not let any relationships happen. He'd had the occasional date when he'd felt lonely. But his one and only true diversion had been Skye, and after that he had battled with the voice inside him, telling him that he should never have done it.

He had been the perfect gentleman since then. Just wanting the pleasure of a woman's company, the conversation without the complications.

Friendship was all he had ever been after. And yet here he was in one of the most complicated situations he'd ever faced!

Lane affected him in a way he'd never thought would be possible again. And he didn't know how to feel about it. It would be so easy to let their relationship happen. He could have the family he'd dreamed of for years.

His body, his heart, wanted that.

But his logical mind screamed at him to stay away.

Which would win? He didn't know, and it was a delicious agony as he drove to Weston with Lane by his side, knowing she was close and that they had the whole day together.

He wanted to give her anything she wanted today. He didn't want the day to be bittersweet, though he supposed it would be, no matter how hard he tried. He wasn't Skye. He never would be. But he was determined to give her the best birthday she had ever had.

'What do you want to do first when we get there?'

She sighed. 'I want to see the sea. It was the first thing Skye and I would always do. We'd go to the promenade, kick off our shoes and run across the beach and paddle in the water.'

'Even today?' It was a little overcast. Not the perfect day for the beach, he had to admit.

She nodded. 'Even today.'

'Okay. And then what?'

She laughed. 'The funfair to play on the games and win cuddly toys.'

'We can do that. I used to be a dab hand at those grabby things.'

'Me too! We ought to have a competition. See who can win the most!'

He smiled. 'All right, you're on. First one to ten doesn't have to buy the fish and chips.'

'But they do get to buy the ice-cream.'

He grinned and nodded. 'Favourite flavour?'

'Mint choc-chip.'

'Mine too!' He laughed, enjoying how easy it was to talk to her even without Tori there.

He'd worried about that. Thought they would have nothing to say to one another. His daughter was the one thing they shared, but without her he and Lane were practically strangers to one another really.

'Have you ever been to Weston before?' she asked.

'Once—for a medical conference. But I was stuck inside a seafront hotel for the whole day, so I never really got to see it properly—though it was all lit up at night when I left.'

'I guess you're used to going overseas for holidays?'

He shook his head. 'Not always. We went to Scotland

once. Spent a weekend in Dublin—though I don't remember too much about that one!' He laughed again. 'What about you?'

'My mum always took me to the seaside each year. Skegness. Yarmouth. The Isle of Wight one year. I've never really travelled.'

'Why not?'

She shook her head. 'I've just never had the opportunity and…um…when I met *Simon* he was always working.'

He heard the way she said his name. The hesitation before. The emphasis. This Simon had meant something to her. 'A boyfriend?'

She glanced at him and nodded her head. 'Unfortunately.'

'Should I change the subject, or…?'

He didn't want to push, even though he was desperate to know more about her. What made her tick? And why had her relationship been unfortunate?

'No. We can talk about it.' She let out a sigh. 'It started as it always does. I thought he was my Prince Charming and in the end it turned out he was just a toad I should have thrown back into the scum-filled pond.'

'Ouch! How long were you together?'

'A year.'

'It was serious, then?'

'The first few months were bliss. Or my infatuation made me think it was bliss. He was handsome. Charming. Delightful to everyone. I asked him to move in with me, because I hated being apart from him, and he kept saying that we were inseparable. It was what I wanted to hear. That someone couldn't live without me. I wanted

to believe him, but I was already making too many ex-
cuses for his behaviour without realising I was doing it.'

He listened. Not just to the words, but to the tone in
which they were said. Her voice said so much that her
words didn't.

'I had a job in a nursing home at the time. It was
stressful…caring for elderly people with dementia. But
it wasn't them—it was the new management that came in
that really made it tough. Simon didn't like how much I
talked about it when I came home, but I was only trying
to blow off steam. I needed him to listen and he didn't
want to.'

'What happened?'

'Skye got sick. I'd been so wrapped up in Simon, so
engrossed by what I thought was love, that I hadn't been
seeing her as often, even though she was coping with
pregnancy by then. He didn't like me spending time with
her, but when she got diagnosed halfway through her
pregnancy I just knew I had to be there for her.'

Cole nodded. 'You were best friends.'

'Exactly. But Simon hated it that someone else had
my attention.'

'What happened?'

'I began going with Skye to her hospital appointments.
That often meant we were out for hours. I hardly saw
Simon, and when we did see each other we argued. He
kept telling me he needed me, too, but he wasn't sick, or
scared the way Skye was. And then she was told it was
inoperable, that the cancer had spread, and she told me
her plans about wanting me to be her baby's guardian.'

'What did Simon have to say about that?'

She laughed bitterly, shaking her head. 'He wasn't best
pleased. Looking after someone else's baby? He didn't

want to be a father. He could never be that selfless. When he discovered I'd already agreed we had a massive fight and he gave me an ultimatum. Him, or Skye and the baby.'

Cole was shocked. He didn't know what to say.

'She had no one but me she could turn to, and no one should ever have to die alone.'

He thought about Andrea. She had died alone.

'Why didn't Skye tell me? That she was pregnant?' he asked.

'She didn't think it was right to tell you. It had been a one-night stand—she couldn't imagine rocking up to your doorstep and telling you she was pregnant, and then telling you that she wouldn't live long enough to see her baby grow up. So she made a decision. Whether it was right or wrong, we can't change that now.'

'I would have liked to know her more.'

'You would?'

'Yes. She sounds like a very caring friend. A gentle soul.'

'She was.'

'I'm sorry this Simon hurt you. You deserve better than that.'

'Thanks.'

They were both quiet for a while. The signs to Weston promenade were now showing on the road as they got closer and closer.

It hurt him to know that Lane had been in such a terrible relationship. If he had been her friend back then, and he'd heard what this Simon had done, he would have gone round there and... What? Punched the guy?

Maybe... He wasn't a violent man, but he would have liked to defend her and let this Simon know in no uncertain terms just how low a life-form he was. He'd certainly sounded like a giant idiot. Selfish and unthinking. He could never treat a woman in such a way.

'Let's forget Simon. Forget ovarian cancer and death and celebrate life. *Your* life. Your birthday. What do you say?'

She smiled at him and gave a single nod. 'Let's do it!'

CHAPTER SEVEN

'READY?'

She beamed a smile at him. It was cold, and the wind was blowing hard now they stood on the exposed beach. It was even beginning to spit a little with rain. 'I am!'

She took her hand in his. 'Then let's go!'

They began running across the sand, the coarseness of it squelching softly between their toes. Some parts were firmer underfoot than others as they ran towards the sea that coursed towards them in low, frothy waves. As their toes hit the icy-cold water Lane squealed at the temperature, hopping over the low waves, water splashing up her legs, before they both stood there panting and staring out to sea.

She felt so amazing! So alive and...

As she stared out to sea, reminding herself that she did not have Skye by her side for the first time ever, she felt tears prick her eyes. Inhaling deeply, determined not to cry, she gazed out across the churning water and wondered if Skye was looking down at her, wishing she could be there, too.

She felt Cole squeeze her hand and she glanced at him in thanks. But he was gazing out at the water, too, as if he knew she needed this moment to remember her friend.

Needed this moment to shed a solitary tear because a new chapter in her life had begun. Without her best friend by her side.

Instead she had Cole by her side.

Who knew that he would be this great?

She remembered how she'd felt that morning a few weeks ago, sitting outside Liberty Point Surgery, not wanting to go in, because she'd felt sure she would find nothing but another greaseball. A charmer, like Simon, who used women for his own selfish needs.

Cole was nothing like that. And he'd proved time and time again that he was caring and kind.

The fact that he was handsome and attractive too...

She smiled. How could she hold that against him?

He was so easy to be with, and she liked it that he was holding her hand, supporting her, doing this with her. Making sure her birthday was still a day to remember. He'd not wanted her to be alone on her special day and that meant something.

'I'm glad you're here with me, Cole,' she said.

He turned to look at her, the wind ruffling the top of his hair. 'I'm glad, too.'

'It's cold, it's spitting with rain, and my feet feel like ice, but that doesn't matter.'

He smiled at her.

She loved his smile.

She went up on tiptoe again, to plant a kiss on his cheek as a thank-you. And there she paused, breathing in the scent of salt against his skin, the slight dampness of his hair, the way he held her against him. She pulled back slightly, looking into his eyes, not sure what she was doing or whether it was wise.

He looked back at her. Did he want her to kiss him?

She thought so. She hoped so. But what if it complicated matters? What they had between them was good at the moment—why confuse matters by kissing him? What if it all went wrong?

She smiled uncertainly and took a step back.

Did he seem relieved? Or upset? She couldn't tell.

'Let's go back,' she said.

He nodded. 'Sure.'

They didn't run back. They walked. Still hand in hand.

She relished the contact. The heat of his skin. The strength of his grip. It was almost as if he was saying, *Don't worry. I've got you. I won't let you go.* She felt safe. Protected by this tall man at her side. She almost didn't want to get back to the promenade, because then she would have to let go of his hand to put on her shoes again. She even slowed her walk so that it would take longer.

Reluctantly, she let go and sat on the wall, so she could brush the sand off her feet and put on her shoes.

He did the same, and then—*oh, yes!*—he held out his hand for hers and they walked towards the arcade.

They sat in the seated area of the fish and chip shop, eating their food, as outside the rain poured in a torrent.

Thankfully, inside it was warm, the air filled with the scent of food and salt and vinegar, and they both filled their bellies with perfectly cooked chips and the crispy thick batter around perfect pieces of meaty cod.

'Why is it that fish and chips always tastes better at the seaside?' Lane asked.

'I don't know. I'm sure there's a suitably confusing mathematical equation, researched by experts after years of study to explain it, but I'm just going to accept the fact that it does.' Cole smiled and dipped a chip into a small pot of ketchup.

Beside them sat a bag of sixteen cuddly toys that they had won from the arcades, and Lane was still quite pleased that she'd made it to ten before he had. They were cheap and tacky, but they'd been fun to get, and she was looking forward to taking them home and putting them in the hammock she had on the wall in Tori's room.

'I'm having a great birthday—thank you.'

'Hey, my pleasure—and it's not over yet.'

'No?'

'No! There's ice-creams to have, and then there's a ride that I think we should go on.'

She almost stopped eating. 'A ride?'

She'd never really liked rollercoasters. She'd ridden some quite tame ones…gone on a log flume once or twice…and she had hated the feeling in her stomach when they had dropped over the side and splashed her with cold water at the bottom.

'After all this food? Is that wise?'

'We'll be fine. Honest. I'll look after you.'

'You'd better.'

He smiled. 'Trust me.'

The rain had begun to clear as they walked towards the funfair. Lane bit her lip, wondering what ride Cole wanted to take her on and what excuse she could use to get out of it!

Part of her wanted to be brave and trust him, but another part of her told her she'd been on enough crazy rides in her lifetime and didn't really need to go on one more!

But she didn't want to be a spoilsport. And she didn't want to ruin the day the way she had once when she'd gone to a fair with Simon and he'd called her a Sulky Sue for not going on a giant rollercoaster.

So she walked beside Cole, her arm slipped inside his, and as they walked through the stalls where you could shoot at playing cards, or hook ducks, or throw darts at balloons she tried to lose herself in the traditional British seaside atmosphere—the noise, the aroma of candy floss and toffee apples and hot dogs with fried onions.

She saw a waltzer, a gentler teacup ride, a big wheel and a helter-skelter. Which ride was he taking her to? The Crazy Mouse? The Robo-Coaster?

'Here we go.'

She looked ahead in disbelief. 'The Ghost Train?'

He laughed at the look on her face. 'What did you *think* I was going to take you on? I can't even manage a carousel without wanting to throw up, and this is meant to be the scariest ghost train in the country!'

She shook her head and then rested it against his arm, feeling a world of relief. 'I can do a ghost train.'

'Let's sit at the front.'

And she laughed again as eagerly, like a child, he clambered into the front car and held out his hand to help her in. She sat beside him and he lowered the bar, securing them into place.

The ride attendant came by and took payment, checked their safety bar and then went to check on the others.

'You like scary rides, huh?' she asked.

'Gotta get that adrenaline rush somehow.'

She slipped her arm into his. 'I'll take care of you.'

'You'd better. I need to drive us home, and I won't be able to do that if I'm traumatised.'

The car slowly began to move forward.

Clack-clack.

From behind the dark doors that slowly opened in front of them they heard howls and ghost noises. Lane reached for Cole's hand and squeezed it as they passed into darkness.

The car twisted to the right, then to the left as skeletons and scary zombies suddenly screeched into the light, looming over them.

Lane gasped, and laughed, and then the car spun crazily to the left again, clattered through more dark doors, and there was an evil clown holding a bunch of burst balloons and reaching for them with spiky teeth. There was a crack of thunder and a flash of lightning and the car was yanked right and propelling them into a tunnel of cobwebs that brushed their faces and made them jump.

She leaned into Cole, laughing, and he leaned towards her. And then everything went dark and the car dipped down a metre or so, making their stomachs plummet, before lifting again as a ghost screeched right in their faces.

She turned to face Cole, to laugh with him, to enjoy this with him, and saw that he was gazing at her, his face full of joy. Suddenly the scary ride was forgotten. The flashes of light, the plunging into darkness, the pretend gore and blood—all gone.

All there was, was Cole. Beyond him the darkness flared with light, and there were figures, but she didn't know what. Didn't want or need to focus on them because of the way he was looking at her. His face flickered in the light, shade and shadow, and his eyes were intense as they gazed back at her...

And suddenly they were back in daylight and the ride had stopped.

His lips touched hers.

She deepened the kiss, welcoming the feel of his tongue in her mouth, allowing herself this moment that she had craved for so long, forgetting all the complicated issues that came with it, forgetting all the cruelty that had befallen them both and not caring whether this was sensible or not. Whether this was wise. All that mattered was him, and the feel of him in her arms, and the fact that right at that moment she didn't want anything else at all.

'Excuse me, can I get on?'

A child's voice broke the spell and they pulled apart. Her cheeks were flushed. She felt breathless and unsure of what to say. The adrenaline in her body wasn't from the ride at all, but from Cole.

The safety bar snapped back and he took her hand and helped her out of the car. They stood there for a moment, staring at each other, not knowing what to say…

Cole had not thought for one moment that he would end up kissing Lane that day. He'd intended to give her a fun day out, to take away some of the sadness that she would be feeling at not having her best friend to celebrate with as usual. The most he'd thought would happen was that he would get to know her a little more and deepen their friendship.

Had he ruined everything?

The crushing wave of guilt that flowed through him once again was familiar. He'd been out with women since his wife's death—just once or twice, when he'd felt he couldn't bear another night in alone—but he'd never done this. Kissed a woman as if he meant it. Kissed her as if he wouldn't be able to breathe unless he did so. Kissed her because he couldn't stop himself.

What they'd had between them would now be changed.

This desire…this yearning he had felt for Lane had slowly been building. He'd tried his best to ignore it, but sometimes you just couldn't fight something like that. It was primal. It was…*life*.

'I'm sorry. I didn't mean to…'

His words trailed off as he stared into her eyes. Her face. Her lips were still parted from their kiss and all he could think of right now was how perfect they had felt. How soft. How good it had felt to kiss her.

'No. It's all right. It was just…the heat of the moment.'

She didn't sound as if she believed herself one bit. Was she trying to let him off the hook?

'We need to keep things professional between us. It… er…' he swallowed hard, unable to stop thinking about that kiss '…won't happen again.'

She nodded. 'Right. No, you're right. It's complicated, isn't it?'

Complicated didn't adequately explain it.

'Yes, it is. So…what do you fancy doing next?' he asked.

He felt bad for trying to change the subject when something so monumental as he and Lane kissing passionately had just happened. It felt cowardly, and that caused even more guilt to come crushing down upon him. He couldn't bear it, so he randomly walked over to a stall and handed over a five-pound note to have a go on whatever that stall was.

It turned out to be a firing range, where little plastic guns were chained to the counter. He loaded the gun with tiny yellow plastic balls. Apparently he had to knock down a trio of dented cans. He aimed and got the first one off with a single shot, but missed all the others. He stared at the cans, at their dented exterior after a thousand hits, and wondered if his soul looked the same?

Happiness always ended in tragedy.

What had he been *doing* to let his feelings emerge like that? Lane was his daughter's godmother! Her legal guardian. If he screwed this up, she could walk away and he'd not be able to do a damned thing about it! Well…

He was meant to be getting to know his daughter—not falling for the woman who was her guardian. Not to mention the fact that they were work colleagues! In a tiny practice! If he ruined this the repercussions could be mighty—not just for him and his future with his daughter, but for his patients, too!

He'd messed with fire and this was the burn. Yes, he'd be lying if he said he hadn't thought about how convenient it would be if they *did* get together—but what if that was all this was and he was mistaking convenience and the promise of a ready-made family for real attraction?

Cole hadn't won anything at the stall, but he wasn't ready to turn away from it and see Lane's face.

What was she thinking? Did she feel rejected? She'd seemed to agree with him that the kiss had been a bad idea…but hadn't she kissed him back? She'd pressed herself against him. She'd run her fingers through his hair and it had felt so good! Were they the actions of a woman who didn't want to be kissed?

Or perhaps she'd been feeling like him? Had just got carried away in the moment and forgotten what really mattered just for a moment of madness? Or maybe she was the one playing him to get a ready-made family?

He turned from the stall and looked at her. Her hair was getting damp from the thin drizzle that was falling and she had no hood on her coat. 'Let's get you a brolly,' he said.

'It's fine.'

'No, it's not. I think I saw some in that gift shop.'

He bought her an umbrella, and because she was so much shorter than he was it gave him a good reason to walk apart from her, so that he didn't get poked in the shoulders by the spikes.

Whatever closeness they'd previously had, it now felt precarious. It was as if there was a wall between them. He knew that the wall was of his own making. But he needed it. That wall had kept him safe since Andrea's death, and right now he needed to reinforce it. To make it clear that Lane couldn't broach it. Look at what had happened the last time he had overstepped it.

Even if the memory of their kiss and how she had made him feel did make him want to rip that wall down brick by brick and cross the line once again...

'Have you two had a falling out?' asked Mary, the receptionist.

Lane had been standing at Reception, just passing the time whilst she waited for her next patient to arrive, when Cole had walked up, passed over some swabs to be sent to Pathology, and then walked away without saying a word.

She had been hyper-aware of him being there. Knew exactly that it had been *his* surgery door that had opened, *his* footsteps she'd heard approaching and had breathed in his cologne as he'd stood by her side to hand the swabs to Mary to put in the collection box.

She'd tensed when he'd stood next to her, even though she'd not meant to. But her birthday had ended so awkwardly, and he'd driven her home practically in silence, only making occasional comments on the rain or the traffic and then saying a hurried, 'Thank you for today,' when he'd dropped her off at her house.

She'd never before needed a hug from Tori so badly! Needed just to hold her and squeeze her tight and talk to her as if she were Skye.

'I made a huge mistake today. I kissed him. I kissed your father. And it was breathtaking and amazing and the whole world stopped turning for just a moment.'

She'd paused then, imagining Skye asking the question, *'And then what happened?'*

And then *nothing* had happened. She'd seen his shutters come down so quickly, and although it had been raining and cold all day, that had been the first time she'd felt a chill. The fun had gone out of the day and they'd both quickly agreed that maybe it was time to go home?

At the start of the day she'd imagined arriving home and thanking him with a big smile and a peck on the cheek, saying, *See you Monday!* as she skipped from the car. But nothing could have been further from the truth. And now she didn't know how to be around him.

'No. Not really,' she said now.

Mary smiled. 'Not *really*? That means you've at least had words of some kind. You can tell me; I won't tell anyone else.'

Lane smiled at Mary's persistence. 'He took me out for my birthday and it didn't go very well, that's all.'

'Oh…' Mary seemed thoughtful. 'How so?'

'It was raining and cold and just not the fun day we'd envisaged.'

'But surely then you'd be commiserating with each other? You froze faster than if you'd been dipped in liquid nitrogen when he came up beside you.' Mary tapped her finger against her bottom lip. 'Something else happened…'

'Nothing happened.'

'You sure of that?'

She smiled. 'Absolutely.' And then she felt a welling of relief as she saw her patient arrive for his free NHS Health Check. 'Mr Jammeh! Would you like to come down?'

As she escorted her patient down the corridor Mary leaned over the reception counter and called after her, 'I'll find out!'

Lane shook her head. She liked Mary. She was like the practice's mother hen, looking after all her chicks.

She opened her door and escorted her patient in.

At the end of the day Lane was just finishing off the last few things she had to do. She'd cleaned and wiped down her room, and now she needed to go into each doctor's room and make sure it had a good supply of blood and urine bottles, that the sharps bins weren't in need of being changed, and to check the bed curtain to see if it needed changing. Shelby, the practice HCA, had left her a check list, which was helpful, and she assumed that as it was late, the doctors all should have left by now to do home visits.

She switched off her computer and checked Dr Summer's room first. It was fine, and all she needed to do was make sure the examination bed had a fresh blue paper cover after wiping it down. After that she did Dr Green's room, knowing in her head that she was deliberately leaving Cole's room till last. Dr Green needed a new box of disposable tourniquets and some new needles.

She checked the nurse's room, to make sure the fridges were locked and secure and all the temperatures recorded in the file. Then she cleaned down the sluice, all the time listening for sounds from outside.

She couldn't hear anybody. No printer running off prescriptions, no typing, no doctor recording notes into a voice recorder.

He had to have gone, right?

With trepidation, she went to Cole's room. The door was shut and she pressed her ear to the wood for just a moment, resting her face against its cool, smooth surface, her eyes closed as she fought to remove the memory of that kiss.

Suddenly the door was pulled open and she almost fell straight into his arms.

'Whoa! You okay?' He dropped his briefcase to catch her, his hands holding tight onto her upper arms.

Blushing madly, she stepped back, freeing herself, straightening her tunic. 'Sorry! I was just about to come in, but I thought I heard you moving around inside and figured you were still working.'

She was babbling, because she didn't know what else to do. She couldn't make eye contact; she didn't feel brave enough for that just yet. They'd not really spoken to each other properly since that kiss, and now he was just standing there, staring at her as if in expectation, so she had to fill the silence.

'I didn't want to interrupt, so if you've still got stuff to do I'll just go—'

'Lane, it's fine. I'm just leaving.' He sounded disappointed.

Her cheeks felt like the surface of the sun. Did he think she'd been eavesdropping? Did he think she'd been afraid to come in?

'Oh, okay. I need to check your sharps bin and…um… anything else you might need…'

He nodded, picking up his briefcase. 'I think I'm out of green needles. Maybe some vacutainers.'

She nodded, heading over to his sharps bin to check it.

This way he can only see my back and not my face, because my face is hotter than it's ever been!

'Is it still okay for me to come over tonight to see Tori?'

The bin did need changing. She clamped down the opening so that it clicked into place. She'd forgotten they'd made a standing arrangement for Cole to come round each evening to see his daughter before bedtime...

Suddenly she had an image in her head of Cole tucking *her* into bed, leaning over to kiss her goodnight and...

Oh, dear God, think of something else!

'Yes.' She nodded rapidly. 'That's fine. As agreed.'

She turned to face him then, feeling that a smile was needed, but she couldn't meet his eyes. That would just be too much. Especially when she thought of how he'd rejected her after the ghost train.

She should have trusted her first instincts regarding Cole. He didn't want her! He was simply there for Tori! She had been a slight distraction for him—a blip—and she guessed he might be feeling guilty because of his wife, because how could she possibly compare with the love of his life?

Men never wanted her. Her dad had left her behind. Simon had wanted to control her.

Perhaps Cole had said the kiss was a mistake because he thought that if he got involved with Lane, it might somehow jeopardise his chances of spending time with Tori? That if he and she got together and then had a falling out...

Wow, I really know how to let my mind run away with itself.

Lane decided the quicker she acknowledged the fact that Cole was just there for Tori and not her, the better.

'I should be home about six,' she said.

'Seven okay? That gives me time to grab a bite to eat.'

'Seven is perfect.' She tried to smile again, but it faded rapidly as he walked away without saying another word.

What had she done? Ruining everything by kissing Cole? She must have been running a fever, or she must be a mad, mad fool, because this was just atrocious! He was never going to back away from his daughter and she'd better get used him spending time with Tori.

Oh, God! Lane was confused. *He* had kissed *her*. Passionately! They'd both been attracted to each other. She had felt the tension in the air, and she'd thought they'd both become lost in the moment, but...

She got Cole a new sharps bin from the storeroom and attached it to his wall, deciding there and then that when she saw Cole this evening she would put him straight as much as she could.

He had to know that anything emotional she showed was real. That she'd just got caught up in the moment of what had been a difficult day.

He had to know.

He *had* to.

CHAPTER EIGHT

TORI WOULDN'T EAT her dinner, much to Lane's dismay. She'd wanted her fed before Cole turned up, but today, it seemed, Tori thought that food was just for throwing onto the floor.

'Tori, no! Don't do that!' She scooped up some sweet potato mash from the floor and then washed her hands beneath the tap before returning to try and get a few spoonsful into her goddaughter. 'Open up—that's it… that's it… *No! Tori!*'

Tori kept turning away from the spoon, clamping her mouth shut, and Lane was beginning to get really frustrated. Why was she being like this? Normally Tori was brilliant at eating. She loved her food—couldn't get enough of it! But today…

'You don't want to eat today? Well, you do realise that you'll probably wake up in the night hungry?'

She used a wet wipe to mop up Tori's face and podgy little hands and wrists, then lifted her from the high chair and put her down on her play mat whilst she cleaned up a bit and wiped down the high chair.

She could feel her frustration building, already predicting a long night ahead when she'd get no sleep because Tori would cry endlessly. And she didn't want to start feeding her at night again, otherwise she'd think it was a new ritual and wake for milk every night.

'Just when I thought I'd got a handle on this mothering lark…' She leaned against the sink and closed her eyes. She'd worked so hard just lately. Trying to be the best mother Tori could have because she didn't have a real one…

A knock at the door broke her reverie.

Cole.

A sigh escaped her, and she dried her hands on a tea towel and went to answer the door. She pulled it open, expecting to see an uncertain, uncomfortable-looking Cole standing there, and that they would suffer a long couple of hours enduring each other's company, but she realised he was looking at her curiously.

'What? What is it *now*, Cole?' she asked angrily, already feeling close to tears. 'Because, quite simply, I've had a difficult couple of days and—'

He bit his bottom lip and managed an embarrassed smile. 'You have something on your cheek and your… erm…' he pointed at her chest '…shirt.'

She reached to her face and at the same time she looked down. Sweet potato. Heat flooded her cheeks in embarrassment and right there and then she felt she really would cry.

She bit her lip in a bid to stop the tears coming, but she couldn't stop the torrent that had clearly decided that now was the perfect time to humiliate her further. She burst into tears, and the fact that she'd been trying to hold them back so hard meant she gave a hiccupping sob and could do nothing but cover her face in shame.

He must have come in, closed the door, because suddenly he was holding her, comforting her, and she sobbed into his chest, wetting his shirt, trying to cry an apology. But he just shushed her gently and held her until her sobbing had subsided to just a few sniffs and hiccups of breath.

She didn't know how long they stood there like there like that, but what she did know was that she wished she could stay there for ever. But she couldn't, could she? Because he didn't want her.

She pushed away from him, wiping her eyes, hating to break the contact but knowing they ought to check on Tori. 'Sorry. I'm so sorry. I don't where that came from.'

'It's okay. Let me make you a cup of tea.'

She waved him away. 'No, it's all right—I can do it. I just need to check on Tori.'

'You check on Tori. I'll make us both a cup of tea.'

She nodded assent and led him into the kitchen, where he crouched down to say hello to Tori, then busied himself opening cupboards and the fridge to find everything he needed to make them both a drink.

With a steaming mug of peppermint tea beside her on the table, she glanced at Cole uncertainly and found him staring at her.

'Penny for them?' He raised an eyebrow and smiled gently. No judgement. Just friendship.

She hated the fact that she'd allowed a distance to build between them. He was a good man, no matter what had happened between them. Yes, he was here for Tori, but maybe he wanted to be her friend, too?

'It got a little too much for me tonight, that's all.'

He nodded. 'I get it. I mean, sweet potato is a tricky beast…'

She smiled at him. He was letting her off the hook.

'Tori wouldn't eat her dinner, and that was the final straw that brought my house of cards toppling down.'

'You're mixing metaphors, but I think I know what you're trying to say. Have you got a banana?'

A banana? What did that have to do with anything?

'Er…yes. Over there—above the fruit bowl.' She had a small hook there, that she could hang bananas from.

'My mum used to tell me that whenever I wouldn't eat my dinner I would get a banana instead, so that I didn't wake up hungry in the night.'

She smiled, imagining him as a small boy. 'But Tori doesn't want to eat anything.'

'Have you tried it?'

'Well, no, but—'

He peeled the banana, broke it in half and handed it to Tori, who grasped it with utter joy and mashed it straight into her mouth.

Lane shook her head in disbelief. 'You've got to be kidding me.'

'Sometimes babies pick up on stress, too. Perhaps she could sense your…unhappiness?'

He was broaching a subject she wasn't happy about him approaching. 'Maybe.'

'Want to talk about it? I'm a good listener.'

'I'm not sure you're the best person to tell.'

'Well, who would you normally talk to about this?'

She sighed. 'Skye.'

'But she's not here.'

No, and he didn't need to remind her about that. Just the thought made tears prick the backs of her eyes again. It had been such a difficult year. Skye's cancer, Simon's ultimatum, all the *loss*, then taking on Tori and finding Cole.

Kissing him.

Being rejected by him.

Feeling used.

Should he be the one she spoke to about this?

'I've lost people, too,' he said. 'Lost what I never expected to lose. My heart. My wife. My unborn child. And then I learned that I'd lost the first few months of Tori's life. Lost the chance of getting to know her mother.'

She swallowed hard. 'You can't miss Skye?'

'I feel cheated of the chance to get to know who she truly was. She was the mother of my child and I feel I should have known her better. Should have supported her as she went through something so terrifying. As a doctor, I could have helped.'

'Her doctors couldn't do anything. It was too far progressed.'

'I know. But I would have liked the opportunity to meet Skye—to look into her eyes and let her know that I would help look after our daughter in the way she would have wanted. Help give her the best life.'

A tear slipped down her cheek and she hurriedly wiped it away. No more tears. Not tonight.

Could Cole give Tori a better life than what Lane could offer? 'Skye would have appreciated that.'

'I guess instead I can tell you.'

He was staring at her. Deep into her eyes. And she couldn't look away. It was intense. Intimate. Daring.

'I'm no fly-by-night, Lane. I'm dedicated. All my life I've wanted two things—to be a doctor and to be a father. This is my second chance; I'm not losing it.'

She stared back. 'But what if we ruin it?'

He frowned. 'What do you mean?'

'I love Tori and she's all I have left of Skye, and…' She couldn't finish the sentence. Couldn't say the words that had just formed properly for the first time in her mind. She was too busy analysing them herself. Thinking of what they meant.

'And…?' He leaned forward.

On the floor between them Tori had finished the banana—except for a few mashed bits around her fingers and thumb. These she ignored, so that she could play with her bricks.

'And… I love her. Like she's my own.' She couldn't voice her true fears.

He pressed his hand over hers on the table. 'We both do.'

She pulled her hand free and got up from the table. 'But you're her real father. Her real parent. Shouldn't she be with you? I'll never have the connection with her that you do.'

He stood. 'You will always be part of her life, Lane.'

She turned, feeling a fire in her belly. 'I've been her everything! I've been her mother these last few months, I was the one who stepped up, I was the one who sacrificed my life! And for what? To feel like this? Like I'm nothing, compared to you? If we shared her, how would that work?'

'We'll find a way.'

She raised a disbelieving eyebrow. 'Tori needs to have her bath now,' she said.

He sighed, clearly realising they weren't going to settle anything. 'Let me do it.'

'You don't know how she likes it.'

'Then I'll learn. Show me.'

So she did. She told him how deep the water needed to be. The right temperature and how to test it properly.

Which toys Tori liked best in the bath. Her favourite flannel with the clown faces on it. How much bubble bath to use.

And he did it. He bathed her. Played with her.

Lane looked on from the doorway, acknowledging to herself that this was what it was going to feel like as Cole took on more.

If she allowed it. It was an uncomfortable feeling.

'I'm just going to tidy up downstairs,' she said as Cole was drying Tori off and putting on her pyjamas. 'I'll get her last bottle ready.'

She went downstairs and picked up Tori's toys, her teddies, her blocks, putting them all away in a box behind the sofa. With everything away, she tried to tell herself that this was what her future would look like when Cole took on more responsibility. Empty and alone. Simon warned her not to do this. To take on a child that wasn't hers.

It was too much—too depressing to think about.

She turned and went back into the kitchen, making up Tori's bottle. It was time for her to go to bed. She guessed he'd want to do that, too. Learn her routines.

Stupidly, she'd never thought this would happen! She'd been so convinced that when she tracked him down she'd find some sleazeball who would dismiss Tori and walk away. But of course he'd not been like that, had he? He was kind and considerate and caring. He was a good doctor. A good friend. She had no doubt that he would be a good father, too.

As her legal guardian, she would always be a part of Tori's life, but what would she actually be? An outsider? A pretender? Someone who Tori came to view as a nuisance, because she wanted to spend time with her biological parent?

Slowly, with heavy feet, she climbed the stairs. At the top he waited for her, with Tori in his arms, babbling happily. A father with his daughter—as it should be. She should be happy for him. But she knew *his* happiness could cause *her* sorrow.

'Can I put her to bed?'

She passed him the bottle. 'Sure. I normally read to her as she drinks her milk.'

'Okay. Does she have a favourite story?'

'I'll show you.' She led him into Tori's room and passed over the book, watching as he lay Tori down with her bottle. Then she stood in the doorway and listened to him as he read the story, doing all the right funny voices and gently closing the book at the end when he realised that Tori was fast asleep.

They both crept out of her room and he half closed the door behind them. 'She must have been tired,' he said.

'She's very good at going to bed. I've never had any trouble with her.'

'It's because you look after her so well. She's a credit to you.'

She nodded, accepting the compliment. 'Thank you. I'm sure you'll find your way with her routines…'

There was a pause and she looked up at him, hopelessly. Closing her eyes in desperation and shaking her head at the unspeakable. Knowing he would understand that she simply had no more words for the pain in her heart and the fear she felt at the possibility of sharing Tori.

'I'm sorry I upset you on your birthday,' he said suddenly. 'At the fair. With the kiss. I didn't mean to imply it was a mistake. I just got scared, that's all.'

Her heart began to pound in her chest. 'I was scared, too.'

'So much has gone before and... I just didn't want to get into a situation where I let you down. Where I failed you. Us getting involved would be...'

She barely heard his words. Standing there so close, staring deeply into his eyes, she could feel herself edging closer and closer, her hands upon his chest...

And then they were kissing!

It was as if neither of them could help it. They were drawn together. Pulled together. Magnetic. Each needing the other. She could feel him beneath her hands, the strong beat of his heart, the solid muscles beneath his skin, the taste of him in her mouth—it was all she could do to remember how to breathe!

She wanted to absorb every ounce of him, feel every inch of him...

Her hands pulled at his shirt, tucked into his trousers, and searched beneath for his hot skin, the taut muscles of his belly, his chest, his back.

She needed his hands on *her.*

She broke the kiss. 'Come with me.'

She pulled him towards her bedroom, reaching for his shirt buttons the second they got inside.

He pulled her top over her head and his lips found her neck, her throat, and she gasped at the feel of his mouth upon her, the slick swipe of his tongue, the quick nip of his teeth. Pleasure and pain...each as intense as the sensation before it.

She could feel his arousal pressed against her and she revelled in it. Wanted it. *Needed* it. Forget everything else—that didn't matter right now. No matter what, she was drawn to him. As if she couldn't stay away. Even when she'd tried to create a barrier between them it had caused her pain and a depression like no other. It was as if she couldn't breathe without him.

They fell onto the bed with her reaching for the buckle of his belt. Did she have a condom anywhere? In her bedroom drawer? She thought there might be one. When she'd lived with Simon she'd always kept a supply in there.

She reached for the drawer. Yanked it open and blindly searched for something that felt like a condom packet. She pulled something out but it was a box of paracetamol. She threw it to the floor and reached in again. Cole was laughing, and this time she was successful.

Biting her lip with joy, she passed it to him and kissed him passionately. 'No surprise pregnancies this time,' she said.

He smiled and kissed her once again. 'Agreed.'

He woke to the sun peeping in through the curtains and a naked Lane spooning against him. She fitted perfectly, and he closed his eyes briefly as he relished the sensation of holding someone he—

Holding someone he *what*?

If it had been a mistake to kiss her, because it had made him scared, then what would *this* do to him?

But he was loath to break the contact. She felt so right in his arms, and last night had been...*wonderful.* He'd lost himself in this woman and it had felt so *good.* How could something that felt so right be a mistake? It couldn't, could it? Perhaps if they just took it slowly...?

Since he'd dropped her off after her birthday he'd felt awful about the way they'd parted. And then, at work, he'd not even been able to *talk* to her. To converse with her even about patients. It had been one of the hardest things he'd ever had to do—and he'd been through some tough things in his life, so that was saying something!

He'd never shut anyone out like that before. Not if he cared for them. If he had feelings for them. And why wouldn't he have feelings for Lane? She was a beautiful, intelligent woman and she was keeping his daughter safe and loved. If anything, she deserved his utmost respect, and he had treated her like a stranger.

At least they had moved past that now. But would she have doubts when she woke? Would she ask him to leave? Would she think he had slept with her to strengthen his connection to Tori?

He lifted his head to look at the clock. Nearly seven a.m. They'd have to get up for work soon. He'd like a shower if he could.

Lane moved slightly as she stirred against him and his thoughts instantly went to whether she'd want to share that shower with him. His hunger for her was not sated. He craved more.

He nuzzled into the back of her neck. 'Morning, sleepy-head.'

She stretched like a cat and then turned to kiss him. 'Good morning.'

'How long do we have?' he asked, thinking of the entirely different breakfast he could have this morning!

Lane glanced at the time. 'Not long enough. I bet she's already awake.'

'I'll go and get her.'

'She'll need a change of nappy.'

'Okay.' He kissed her on the tip of her nose and smiled at her. 'Are you okay? After last night?'

She nodded. 'More than okay. Are you?'

'I'm good.'

He gave her one last kiss and then threw back the covers and grabbed his boxers, pulling them on.

'Will you get her breakfast ready?'

'Yep. Do you want anything?'

'Whatever you're having is fine by me.'

She smiled. 'Jammy toast?'

'Sounds perfect.'

He went to get Tori and found Lane had been right. She was awake and gurgling away at her bunny in the corner of her cot.

Was this what it would be like to have a family? It felt right. But what if they were pushing things by making a giant leap like this? Yesterday they'd barely been talking and now... There was no going back now, was there?

But I feel happy right now. Why would I want to go back?

Because the last time you were happy it ended in tragedy.

He changed his daughter's nappy and carried her downstairs. His heart melted when she lay her head against his chest. She was such a loving little girl, with no idea yet of her sad history. Lane was doing a wonderful job, raising this little girl to be happy and bright despite how she must be feeling in dealing with the grief of her best friend's passing.

The smell of coffee and toast made his stomach rumble and he slid Tori into her highchair. Lane had already placed there some dry cereal, fruit and toasted soldiers, along with a bottle of milk.

'Can I help?'

She smiled at him and he loved the way she looked in the morning. Ruffled and sleepy and content.

'Everything's under control,' she said.

He poured some milk into his coffee and took a sip. Perfect! 'I have to leave soon.'

She turned at the counter, looking concerned. 'Oh? Why?'

'I can't turn up to work in the same clothes I left in. Mary would spot that a mile off.'

Lane relaxed a little. 'Okay.'

'I really enjoyed last night,' he told her.

'Me too.'

'Good. But we're going to have to be careful at work.'

She sat down at the table next to him, biting into a slice of toast. 'In case people notice that we're friends again?'

He reached for her hand. 'I think we might be more than that now.'

She smiled. 'Maybe...'

'And if Mary can spot that we're not talking to each other, she'll certainly spot that I'm looking at you in a different way.'

'In what way?'

'A way that says I've seen you naked and I'd like to see you that way again.' He grinned.

Lane covered Tori's ears and laughed. 'Shh... Not in front of the baby!'

CHAPTER NINE

LANE WAS IN a cheery mood when she dropped Tori off at her mother's house—so much so that her mum even commented on it. She tried to tell her that she'd just had a really good night's sleep, but she could tell her mum wasn't fooled. She would have to be much better at hiding her feelings when she got to work?

The sun was shining over Liberty Point Surgery when she arrived, and she spotted Cole's car already in the car park. She parked next to it and headed into work with a bright smile in place.

'Morning, everyone! Morning, Mary.' And there he was. 'Good morning, Dr Branagh!' she added as she passed him in the small kitchenette to get to the kettle.

'Good morning, Lane. How are you today?'

She smiled back. 'Very well, thank you. You?'

'I'm good!' he said, and headed off to his room.

And Lane smiled like the cat that had got the cream.

Mary came in, looking at her carefully. 'Okay, what's going on?'

She tried to look innocent. 'What do you mean?'

'You could barely look at each other yesterday and today you're all smiles like…' Mary paused as a thought struck her. 'Are you and he…*courting*?'

'Us?'

Mary grinned. 'I knew it! I knew it the second I saw you walking in here like everything's wonderful, sunshine and roses—and he hasn't shaved either!'

Lane tried to look puzzled and not to blush. 'I don't get you. What's him not shaving got to do with anything?'

'Well, clearly he had enough time to go home and get changed, but not enough time to have a shave. Dr Branagh has *never*—not once—turned up to work with anything less than a clean shave, *and* he has a twinkle in his eye and a spring in his step that I haven't seen since...' Her eyes darkened. 'Well, since Andrea...'

At the mention of Cole's dead wife the smile left Lane's face. 'You mustn't tell anyone, Mary. It's complicated.'

'Oh, lovey, it's *always* complicated. That's the nature of love.'

'Well, I don't know if we're *there* yet.'

Mary grabbed her mug from the kitchenette cupboard and grinned. 'I do.'

'You're hopeless! A hopeless romantic!'

'Well, in my day romance meant something. These days it's all sex and lust. Not that there's anything wrong with that—but in my experience it doesn't last. Love does.'

'Does it?'

Lane wasn't sure. She'd thought Simon had loved her the way she'd loved him and what had happened there? He hadn't been able to bear to share her at all. Had tried to isolate her. Given her cruel ultimatums and then blamed her when their relationship collapsed.

Was she being foolish, falling for Cole's charms? Naïve? Was she re-enacting history once again? Doomed to fail and never to measure up?

What if this relationship failed? If they even had a relationship! They'd spent one night together. Had that been lust? Or romance?

I don't know. Can't it be both?

'Love endures all things,' said Mary. 'What's that quote that says all couples who are meant to be are the ones who go through all the rubbish designed to tear them apart but come out so much stronger than anyone could ever imagine?'

Lane shrugged. 'I don't know. Is it in The Bible?'

Mary laughed. 'No, lovey—I think it was a meme on social media.'

She couldn't help but laugh, too. The idea of Mary being au fait with what was happening on the internet seemed odd. It didn't seem her thing.

But then Mary got serious. 'I like you, Lane, but I've known Dr Branagh for much longer and I know what he's been through. He doesn't need any more turmoil in his life. He doesn't need any more grief. Please don't cause him any. He's a good man.'

'I know he is. I won't hurt him, Mary. I promise.'

'Good. Now, then, let's get those doors open and let our patients in. We've got some work to do.'

Lane welcomed in her first patient—an elderly lady of seventy-two who was there for a hypertension review.

Lane greeted her and indicated that she should sit down. 'How have you been, Mrs Walker?'

'Just fine! As far as I know!'

'Been taking your medication regularly?'

Mrs Walker nodded.

'No headaches, nosebleeds?'

'None at all.'

'That's good. And have you been keeping track of your blood pressure at home? You have your own machine, don't you?'

'Sometimes I forget, but it's generally all right. Here's my last set of readings.'

She passed over an A4 sheet of paper with her blood pressure readings taken each morning and night. They were generally a little higher than Lane would like, but weren't sky-high.

'We'll do a blood test today—is that all right?'

'Of course. Anything you have to do.'

Lane began to gather the equipment she would need.

'I hear that you have a little one? A baby girl—is that right?'

'Er…yes…'

'Someone told me that her father is Dr Branagh?'

Lane froze. What had Mrs Walker heard? And who was talking about them?

'I'm sorry?'

'I don't mean to interfere, and it's really none of my business, but I do admire Dr Branagh so much. And when his wife died… Well, I'm sure you understand. To find out that he has a child after all is…' Mrs Walker searched for the right words.

Atrocious? A scandal? Gossip for the grapevine?

'Just wonderful for him. He so deserves happiness.'

Lane nodded. 'So does everyone else.'

Why was everyone so concerned about Cole's happiness? What about hers? *She* wanted to be happy, too!

'Could you roll up your sleeve for me, please?'

Lane performed the blood test and then used the patient's other arm to take a blood pressure reading. It was still a little high. One hundred and forty-two over one hundred and one. But perhaps Mrs Walker was excited about all the gossip? Or nervous about the blood test? Only she hadn't seemed nervous...

'We'll do another reading in a moment.' She tapped her assessment into the computer. 'What sort of exercise are you getting each week, Mrs Walker?'

'I do a bit of walking. To the shops and things.'

'Anything else?'

'Not really.'

'You don't smoke, do you?'

'Not any more. I used to, years ago.'

'And what about your diet? Do you use a lot of salt in your cooking?'

'A bit. And I do like to add some to my meal when it's on the plate.'

'Maybe you could consider cutting down? Even if you just start off by not putting it on your meals at weekends?'

Mrs Walker considered it. 'I could, I suppose...'

Lane took Mrs Walker's BP for a second time and saw that it had come down slightly—which was better, even if it wasn't great.

'We'll use this lower reading. So, I'll get your bloods sent off and if you don't hear from us assume everything's normal.'

'All right. Is that it? Am I done?'

'You're all done.'

She smiled and watched as Mrs Walker began to amble her way from the room. The burning question broke free before she could stop it.

'Can I ask...how did you hear about Tori being Dr Branagh's daughter?'

The woman stopped at the door. 'I heard it from my

friend Alice. But I think she heard it from *her* friend…
erm… Caroline, I think…'

So it seemed their little secret was definitely out, then?
Someone must have heard about Tori. Had Cole said anything? He might have told his parents? Did he even *have*
any? And if they'd told people…

'Right. Okay.'

'We all think it's wonderful. He deserves happiness
after all he's been through.'

So you said.

Lane smiled and nodded. 'See you next year, Mrs
Walker,' she said, even though she knew she wasn't going
to be here for very much longer. Shelby would soon be
back and Lane and Tori would be long gone.

Unless…

Did she dare think that she might have a chance at a
future with Cole? Was he even on the market for another
relationship? Could she measure up to what he'd had with
his wife? What would it mean, sticking around here? She'd
get to keep Tori in her life, that was for sure, and Cole?
She really did like the idea of keeping Cole in her life.
But that would only be if she could believe he was nothing like the other men in her life. Like *Simon.*

She crossed her fingers without even thinking about
it. Touched the wood of the chair opposite her.

Lane would take all the luck she could get.

Later she and Cole drove to the park, put Tori in her buggy
and began to walk, hoping to find a nice spot. It seemed
lots of other people had had the same idea, and the park
was filled with sunbathers and families enjoying an ice
cream.

In the centre of the park there was a small café, and

next to it a small aviary filled with beautifully coloured budgies and canaries up high and ground quails on the floor below. There were lots of toddlers gazing in and squealing at the birds, which fluttered and flew about at each noise.

'There's a space over there.'

Cole pointed to a space where they could lay their picnic blanket and they headed over the grass to claim the spot. Behind them was a small flowerbed, filled with roses and edged with lavender, thick with busy bumblebees.

Lane laid out the blanket and then set about unloading the picnic she'd packed. There were sandwiches and sausage rolls, grapes and fruit, yoghurt, rice cakes, pâté and crackers. Simple fare that would be easy to snack on.

'Did I tell you we've become quite the talking point?' she asked.

Cole raised an eyebrow. 'Us?'

'Well, more you. And Tori. People know she's your daughter.'

'And they think you're her mum?'

'No. They seem to know I'm not. God only knows what explanation they've come up with for that.'

Cole shrugged his shoulders as he helped put some food into a small bowl that had a suction cup on the bottom, so Tori couldn't throw it to the ground from her buggy tray.

'We know the truth. That's what matters.'

'It doesn't bother you that people are talking about you behind your back?'

He shook his head. 'No. Not really. They talked plenty when I lost Andrea. You can't stop gossip, can you?'

'But they could be saying the wrong thing! What if they assume you had an affair while you were married?'

'Then Tori would be much older than she is. I can only hope and pray that my patients' mathematical skills are as acute as I would like them to be.' He popped a grape into his mouth and made an appreciative sound. 'These are good.'

He stuck the bowl to Tori's tray and waited for the little girl to start eating, then sat back cross-legged on the blanket.

'Does it bother you?' he asked.

She looked down at the ground, loath to admit that it did. Simon had spread some awful rumours about her after she'd chosen Skye and Tori over him.

'It does, doesn't it? Why?'

'I once had a big group of friends. My own… Simon's. When we split we were the hot topic. It was hard to go anywhere afterwards because of it. People took his side. People I'd thought would have my back. I tried to tell them the truth, but Simon was a very effective storyteller.'

'They shut you out?'

'It was like I'd had an affair.'

'People act weirdly in situations they don't fully understand.'

Suddenly Tori let out a cry, and Lane whipped her head round to look and saw a bee fly away from Tori's face. Had she been stung?

'Oh, my God! Tori!'

She scrambled to her feet at the same time as Cole and tried to look at the baby's face, but it was hard because Tori was crying and her face was red and blotchy.

'Did it sting her? Where did it get you, sweetie? Tell

me…show me where it hurts.' She turned to Cole. 'What if we need ice?'

'She'll be okay. We don't know if it stung her. Besides, it flew away—don't bees die after they lose their sting?'

'I don't know. Why won't she stop crying?' Lane was jiggling her up and down, trying her best to soothe her.

'Here, let me try.'

Cole took Tori from her arms and began to gently sway her from side to side, but there was a look on his face that alarmed her.

'What is it?'

'Her face is beginning to swell.'

'That's the sting, right?'

'Could be… But there's also the flushing and… Are those hives?'

Lane tried to see, but it was hard. 'I don't know.'

'Let me listen to her breathing. Take her pulse.'

'Oh, come on—it can't be that bad.'

'Was Skye allergic to bee stings?'

Lane stopped, her blood chilling at a long-forgotten memory. 'There was a wasp sting once… The swelling lasted a few days, but she didn't get seriously ill or anything!'

Cole's face showed deep concern as he listened to Tori's laboured breathing.

'Call an ambulance. *Now!*'

CHAPTER TEN

HE'D THOUGHT THEY'D be having a lovely picnic in the park, enjoying being part of their new, weird family unit, but instead he was standing at the bedside of his daughter as a strange doctor injected her with epinephrine.

Her anaphylaxis had been rapid onset and had affected her breathing. The paramedics, when they'd arrived, had thankfully had a pen they could use to inject Tori with, and the doctors had given her another dose. Her pulse was getting stronger, but she was unconscious still and he felt awful. Helpless.

He couldn't lose Tori the way he'd lost Andrea and their baby. He hated feeling helpless, knowing that Mother Nature had struck his family yet again.

Why was this happening to them?

Was he doomed? Cursed? Destined to lose everyone the second he got close to them? The second he gave someone his heart, fate thought it was fair game to rip it out of his chest for a bit of fun?

'This is all my fault,' he said.

'No, No, it's not. It's mine. I should have remembered… considered… But it had never happened before, I…'

He looked at Lane on the opposite side of the bed. Both of them, despite their training, had gone into a panic with no EpiPen in sight, no medical equipment that could help them, no convenient doctor's surgery with its whole stock room in an emergency. They'd been ordinary people, with a just a phone and fear in their hearts at watching a loved one almost slip away.

'We could have lost her,' he said.

'We didn't.'

'But we could have. We should have been better prepared.'

Lane shook her head. 'How were we to know?'

He didn't want to say it, but… 'When Skye had her reaction, what happened?'

Lane looked blank. 'I don't know. I wasn't there. It happened when she was a lot younger.'

'But you'd been friends since you were small?'

'Yes. But it didn't happen when she was with me. It was on a day trip with the children's home, or something. I just remember her telling me about it once. An offhand comment about seeing the doctor because her leg had swelled up so badly she could hardly walk. I just assumed she'd had a bad reaction to the sting—I couldn't possibly have known that her daughter would be severely allergic!' She stared at him. 'You don't blame me, do you?'

He shook his head. 'Of course not! I'm just trying to get this straight in my head—there's nothing like this in my family medical history.'

The doctors with them issued an instruction to the nurses present to keep a watchful eye on Tori, then the lead doctor turned to Lane.

'She's had a bad shock, but she's getting better. We've stopped the main reaction and I'm very sure she'll wake up soon. We'll keep her on oxygen until she does, and the nurses will keep an eye out and make sure you go home with an EpiPen or two for future incidents.'

Cole raised an eyebrow. 'Future incidents? We're never letting her outside again!'

The doctor smiled. 'Everyone reacts like that, but she'll be okay. It just takes time to adjust to a new normal, that's all.'

'Thank you, Doctor. You're sure she'll wake up soon?' asked Lane.

'Absolutely. Her body shut down briefly, but all her vitals are coming back up to normal. You just sit and wait. I'll be around if you need a chat.' He patted Lane on the shoulder and then went on to his next patient.

Cole reached out for Tori's hand and grasped it in his own. It seemed so small and delicate. Like a rag doll's.

He brought it to his lips and kissed it. 'I'm never letting go again.'

Lane didn't want to leave Tori's bedside. She felt that if she took her eyes off her for even a second then something terrible would happen—like it had in the park.

If I'd been paying attention to Tori instead of worrying about gossip, for goodness' sake!

It was haunting to be back in a hospital. The last time she'd been in one it had been with Skye, hearing a doctor tell her that there wasn't any more they could do.

But Tori was breathing normally again. Her airway was clear, her skin was beginning to settle down from the bright red it had first become, and her observations on the monitor were practically normal.

Tori made a noise in her sleep, her eyelids flickering. 'She's dreaming.'

'I hope they're good dreams,' Cole said.

They could still see the indentation on Tori's neck where the bee sting had been, just under her chin. It was like a marker, pointing out their failure to protect her from harm. Lane still couldn't believe she hadn't considered the bee any danger. Wasn't she supposed to be Tori's guardian? Guardians *guarded*. They protected. And Lane hadn't done her job properly.

'Me, too.'

The nurse had brought them a cup of tea, but the drinks sat cooling on the side, both of them unwilling to take their eyes off Tori for a minute.

'At least we'll know going forward. And we'll have medication on hand in case of emergencies.'

Lane nodded. 'We'll have to make sure that when she starts nursery they have one in stock, too. Or should it be two?'

'It's two.'

'Right…'

'I guess one of us is going to have to stay overnight with her.'

Lane volunteered. 'I'll do it. You have work in the morning. I don't.'

'Will you be all right?'

She smiled. 'I have plenty of doctors at my beck and call, if needed.'

'Let's hope they're not. I feel awful at leaving her. What if she wakes and I'm not here?'

'She'll have me.'

She didn't see the look on his face. The one that said he wanted her to have *him*, too. 'You'll call me if anything changes?'

'Of course.'

He got up from his side of the bed and walked round

to her, taking her in his arms. For a moment they stood together, holding each other, taking comfort. It felt good to be in his protective arms again, and she couldn't imagine ever wanting to let go. But his patients needed him. He had a full clinic tomorrow.

She closed her eyes as he kissed the top of her head and squeezed her once more. 'I can be here at a moment's notice. Keep me updated, won't you?'

'Promise.'

They kissed goodbye and he kissed Tori on the cheek, whispering something she didn't catch in her ear. And then he grabbed his jacket and he was gone.

She watched him leave, knowing how hard it must be for him to do so.

Lane settled back beside the bed and lay her head on her elbows. She would watch Tori until she fell asleep herself.

'She's up, she's happy, and she's demolishing her breakfast.'

Cole listened to Lane's happy and very much relieved voice on the other end of the phone. He was so glad! He'd barely slept a wink the night before, only getting about an hour's worth after coming home from the hospital. He'd hated leaving Tori and Lane behind. He'd felt as if he was deserting them.

Today was the first day in his entire life that he really didn't want to be at work. Usually he was happy to go in, with a spring in his step, ready to see how he could help people that day. Even after losing Andrea and the baby he'd only had a few weeks off, and had returned to work feeling brighter and ready to work, welcoming the distraction.

But today he wasn't thinking about work. He was

thinking about how he'd nearly lost his little girl when he'd only just found her. How the doctors wouldn't have been able to tell him anything without Lane being there because he had no legal rights to Tori at all. No rights about her care...her welfare.

His time with Tori had been working out great. She wasn't afraid of him, she gave him cuddles, wrapping her little arms around his neck in a big squeeze that made his heart sing. She smiled when he came into the room and sat down beside her to play. She shared her toys with him, let him feed her, bathe her, put her to bed—all the things a real father would do.

He never wanted to lose that. *Ever.*

But she was in good hands. The hands of doctors. In a hospital. And Lane was by her side and she'd done a damned good job of keeping her safe and healthy so far—though he knew she felt guilty for not suspecting there might be an allergy to bee stings.

What was scary was how rapid onset the symptoms had been. How quickly Tori had gone from crying at the pain of the sting to almost losing her airway and passing out.

He never wanted to feel that scared again. That helpless. Never wanted to feel so lost. Surely it was time he looked into the possibility of making his relationship with Tori official? Make plans for the future? He knew he'd have to ask Lane, but he felt sure she'd be fine with it...

His first patient was Marcus Darby, who was in for a chat about his mental health. Marcus had been struggling of late, and Cole had upped his medication dosage and arranged counselling and cognitive behavioural therapy to get Marcus to cut down on some of his OCD rituals.

'How's it going today, Marcus?'

'Not bad, Doctor. Not bad. It only took me about twenty minutes to leave the house this time.'

'Twenty minutes? That's good. How long did it take you before?'

'A good hour, once I'd finished checking everything.'

'And what do you find yourself checking?'

'That the cooker is off. That the lights are off and the front door is locked properly.'

'How many repetitions are you doing?'

'Ten of each. I've cut down, though, so I'm happy with that.'

'So, do you think the counselling is helping?'

'A bit. She's made me see how my thinking is a vicious circle, feeding each behaviour, and she's given me some different ways to think about my rituals, so they cause me less panic.'

'That's good—good that you understand repeating the same behaviours over and over again may *seem* like a safety belt, but in fact what they're doing is tying you up more and more, trapping you in a cycle.'

'Exactly. I'm not trying to cut the behaviours out completely, but I'm getting them down to a manageable level first, before taking the next step.'

'And you've not replaced old behaviours with new ones?'

Marcus shook his head. 'No. I don't think so. I notice when new worries start up and I talk to myself out loud, with alternative opposite thoughts, until they seem less worrying.'

'So you're able to help yourself? That's good progress, Marcus. You should be proud.'

'Thanks, Doc.' He smiled.

'So you're happy to carry on as you are at the moment? You don't feel the need to change your dosage again?'

'I'm happy as it is. Maybe later, when I'm better, we can look at reducing.'

'One step at a time. Let's not rush this. It's easy to drop back into old habits if we move too fast.'

'All right. Well, thanks, Doc, it was good to see you again.' He reached out to shake Cole's hand.

Cole bade him goodbye and started writing up his notes into the system. When he was done, he checked his phone to make sure there weren't any messages from Lane.

He missed her. Missed having her close. Having her in the next room. For the last few weeks they'd been getting close, and though that had been a scary prospect at first, and he'd almost backed away at one point, now he could see just how much he'd needed her lately. Her being close by made him feel better. The touch of her hand. Her beautiful smile. The way she would try to cheer him when he was feeling blue.

It had been a long time since he'd had someone care for him like that. No one since Andrea, anyway.

It felt good to have that back. A partner. Someone with the same goals as him. A shared purpose.

His feelings for Lane had intensified of late, and although it scared him to think about what that might mean, he kept telling himself that it was okay. As long as they just took it one day at a time and didn't think too much about what the future held, then they could carry on as they were.

He didn't think she wanted anything more from him than that and that was good—because he wasn't sure just how much of himself he had to give. Because giving all his heart was too big an idea for him to contemplate right now.

She had some of it—he knew that. His feelings for her had got bigger and bigger with each night they'd spent together and each morning waking up in each other's arms, but…all of it?

That was too scary to contemplate.

That was too much.

He wouldn't admit anything more—not even to himself.

Day by day—that was all they needed to do.

And when he went to the hospital later he would take Tori a huge teddy bear.

He checked his phone again before admitting his next patient.

'She can go home.'

Cole froze, checked the doctor's face to make sure he wasn't joking. 'You're kidding? Already?'

'Her airway is clear; her observations are normal. She's eating and drinking well, passing urine and faeces—there's no reason to keep her here.'

'But…'

But it's unsafe out there.

The doctor seemed to understand. 'I know it's a scary prospect, but you're forewarned and therefore forearmed this time. You have her emergency kit—she'll be fine… let her live her life.'

'You mean don't keep her cooped up indoors?'

The doctor nodded. 'The temptation to do that—to wrap her in cotton wool—will be strong, but you must try to ignore it.'

Cole thought of his patient Marcus, and why he performed all his safety behaviours to get rid of the worrying thoughts in his head, and began to understand him even more. 'Okay...'

'You know where we are—and our doors are never closed.'

'Well, let's hope we never have to walk through them again.'

The doctor smiled, talked them both through the correct use of her emergency medication once again. and then left them to pack up their belongings and leave. It was amazing how much stuff they'd accumulated. Not to mention the giant teddy bear, almost as big as Cole, that he'd carried in just an hour ago.

Lane gave him a hug, then kissed him. It felt good to get her reassurance. Her affection.

'We'll be okay. I'm sure of it,' she said. 'We'll tackle this one day at a time.'

He was reassured that she was thinking the same way as him. He nodded, and gathered all of Tori's bags and her medication, and Lane sat the teddy bear on the back of the buggy as she pushed Tori towards the exit and home.

As they got to the front doors he felt a brief moment of pure terror, imagining that every bee in the world would somehow know that his daughter was vulnerable and come buzzing down from the skies, but when they emerged and nothing happened he relaxed a little. Not much, but enough.

When Lane took his hand and squeezed it tightly he knew that she'd felt the same thing, and he looked to her with gratitude. They were in this together. He felt that implicitly. They both had the same goal and that was to keep Tori safe, happy and loved.

One day at a time.

They'd promised not to wrap her in cotton wool and to live normally, but it was natural that they would be over-protective, and over the next couple of days they pretty much stayed in, popping out only to go to the supermarket.

Of course Cole was going to work every day, but he was rushing back to her house at night, to spend precious hours with Tori before bed.

Once, he didn't get to see her at all, as he had to go on a home visit one evening that turned into an emergency, meaning he'd gone with his patient to the hospital and waited until the patient's family arrived.

'You're a good man, Cole,' Lane had said, kissing him on the cheek when he'd finally come round late and passing him a longed-for cup of tea.

'I try... I know what it's like to be in hospital alone— and he was so nervous, waiting to see if he'd had a stroke or not. I couldn't walk away. It was my duty to stay.'

'And had he?'

Cole nodded unhappily. 'Afraid so. But he's in the best place now and he'll get great care there. The stroke team are excellent—I've had a few patients taken care of very expertly there.'

'Good. Now you're here, though, you can relax.' She reached for his tie and pulled it loose, unbuttoned the top button of his shirt and went on tiptoe to give him a kiss. 'Let me run you a shower.'

He groaned. 'Sounds wonderful. Thank you.'

'I could make it even better...' she said, with a cheeky smile.

'How so?' He raised an eyebrow.

'I could join you.'

'Well, forget the cup of tea—that sounds even more perfect.'

She started the shower and stood in front of him in the bathroom, slowly stripping him of his clothes, leaving only a smile.

As each piece of clothing was removed she allowed her hands to trace the musculature of his body as more and more of it was revealed. Then she began to take off her own clothes, and then she led him into the spray of water and steam.

She brushed his skin with soft, feather-light kisses, feeling his arousal grow and grow against her body. It was a potent feeling, knowing that *she* was doing that to him. That *she* had that power. That control. Could get that reaction from him.

He reached for her, pulling her closer, grinding her against him, and she smiled and sealed her lips against his in a deep, exploring kiss.

In the heat of the water and the heat of their bodies they allowed themselves to be consumed by the fire they felt within. These last few days they'd both been so stressed, with what had happened to Tori, and they'd been so confined by their fears. But now, with their daughter safely in bed, fast asleep, they could let out all the tension they'd been experiencing and enjoy the softer, more desirous side of life.

Lane moved against him, her soapy body pressed to his, feeling his hands upon her body, urgent and needful.

She groaned with pleasure and searched out his mouth, explored it with her tongue.

This man was all she needed right now.

And feeling this content. This happy...

When had she ever felt this way? She'd thought she had once, with Simon, but that had all been a lie. There'd been doubts with him even at the beginning, and she'd felt afraid for their future. She'd not been able to put her finger on it, and she'd put it down to it being her first ever long-term relationship. She'd been finding her feet... Learning... Not knowing if what she was doing was right, but hoping it was anyway.

But she'd got in too deep, too quickly. She'd had time to think since then. Now Lane was older, wiser, more cautious.

She had been terrified to take this step with Cole, knowing the complications of it, but it seemed to be working. He was a good man. Dedicated. Loving. Considerate of her and her feelings. He didn't seem to be with her just because it was good for his ego, nor did it seem that he was using her. She genuinely thought that Cole was with her because that was what he wanted. Not just because she came with Tori attached and to get access to one, he needed the other.

Yes, she was sure of it. As sure as her previously broken heart could be. And perhaps it was time for her to accept living in the present and forget about what the future held?

There came a time when you just had to make a leap of faith and trust in your instincts, and that was what she was doing now. She paused, remembering the fortune-teller's words, and smiled. Yes, she wanted to keep Cole in her life. He'd become so important to her and she couldn't imagine a future without him.

But right now was for having fun. Right now was for letting off steam and enjoying each other's bodies. No doubt they would dry each other off, go to bed and make love there, and in the morning she would wake in his arms again.

Life was almost perfect.

And she would do everything she could to make sure it stayed that way.

'Lane? If you're free could you pop into my room? I've a patient who might need a dressing—I thought you could give her a once-over.'

'Sure!'

She was just finishing another dressing, for a patient with a diabetic leg ulcer. She washed and dried her hands, entered the details of the wound assessment and the dressings used into the template on the computer, and went to see what she could do next door.

Cole's patient was an elderly lady with a bad cut to her leg.

'Oh, my goodness, how did you manage that?' Lane asked.

'In the garden. I had a fall and caught my leg on the chicken wire that sticks out from the chicken coop.'

'You have chickens?'

'Rescued ones. From those horrible farms they keep them in.'

'Oh, well… Well done, you. Right—let's have a little look at this, shall we? Are you prescribing any antibiotics?' Lane asked Cole.

She was worried about how dirty the chicken wire

might have been. She had no idea of what kind of germs and bugs dirty wire might be covered in.

'Not straight away. And tetanus status is up to date. So, let's dress it and see how it goes.'

'All right. I'll grab something to clean this first and then get some dressings on it. Wait here.'

She came back a moment later, and once they had the patient on the examination bed, raised to a suitable level for their backs, they began dressing the wound, with Lane doing the main work and Cole passing her tape and scissors and entering the details onto the practice system.

'There you go. All done. Tell Mary on the front desk we want to see you again in three days for a re-dressing. Twenty-minute appointment. But if it begins to feel odd before then, or you get hotness or pain, you call us straight away—okay?'

Lane pressed the button the bed that would lower it back down.

'Oh, thank you. You've both been so kind.'

'No problem at all. I'll leave you to it,' Lane said to Cole, and headed back to her own room to await her next patient, who was coming to have some staples removed after knee surgery.

As she sat at her own computer, to see if her patient had arrived yet—he had—she suddenly felt dizzy. It hit her like a wave. She gasped and had to hold her head to keep it steady, to try and fight what her inner ear told her was happening even though in reality it wasn't. She felt nauseous, and a cold, clammy sweat crawled over her. And then, as suddenly as it began, it disappeared.

She released her head carefully and blinked steadily, moving her head from side to side tentatively to see if it would come back. Nothing. Lane looked at the time on her computer. She hadn't eaten for hours. It had to be low blood sugar. She'd not had time to eat her breakfast that morning.

Dipping into her bag, she found a protein bar and ate that, and instantly felt better.

She called in her patient and examined his knee. It had healed very well. The wound was neat and dry, with no redness, no swelling, and no sign of residual infection, but stooping over him she could tell that her head still felt a little...*swimmy.*

Perhaps she was tired? Or maybe she had an ear infection? She'd been through a lot of stress lately with Tori, and perhaps she'd been working too hard? When had she last had a proper break?

It was hard, working almost full-time and looking after a baby, too. She'd been putting her own needs second to those of Tori, and to some degree Cole's too. And they'd been keeping each other awake at night—in the best possible way, of course!—but sometimes you just needed to sleep and get that full eight hours!

She decided to tell him that tonight they must just sleep. Maybe cuddle. But that was it. And that would be nice.

She smiled at the thought as she removed the staples in her patient's knee. 'This last one might pinch. It's very close to the edge of the wound.'

But her patient barely moved, and soon it was all done. She put a much smaller dressing over it as a temporary measure.

'Just leave this on for today, and then you can remove it. Take it easy over the next few weeks, and any problems, come straight back, okay?'

'Will do. Thanks.'

She waved him goodbye at the door and watched him

walk easily down the corridor towards the waiting room. Finally! Her morning clinic was done!

She covered the examination bed with fresh paper after wiping it down, and then settled down upon it—just to close her eyes for five minutes.

A cat nap… That was all she needed, and then she'd be back to normal working order for this afternoon.

CHAPTER ELEVEN

THE PASTA WAS bubbling away in the pot and she had garlic bread slowly going crispy in the oven. Cole was entertaining Tori whilst she prepped and cooked her own homemade tomato and basil sauce. Fresh tomatoes, garlic and basil, a splash of Worcester sauce, a couple of mushrooms and a chopped pepper. Simmering to perfection until it was ready. She served it with a grating of parmesan over each dish, yawning as she did so.

'Tired?' asked Cole.

'A little bit.'

'Maybe you should get an early night? I'll do the dishes and sort Tori out tonight. You go up. Read a book. Relax.'

'Oh, I couldn't do that.'

'Why not?'

She smiled. 'Well… Tori. She's my responsibility.'

'I'd like her to be mine, too. Let me take the reins. We've not spent much time on our own. When we've finished dinner go on up. Warm bath. Pyjamas. Sleep.'

She really did like the sound of that. It was so tempting… 'You wouldn't mind?'

'Course not! In fact, I'd love it. Not that I don't want to spend time with *you*, but me and my girl can have some one-to-one time.'

She crunched down on a piece of garlic bread. 'Okay. I accept your kind offer, good sir.'

'Great! And, if it's okay, I thought after dinner I could take Tori out in her buggy, for a walk.'

'As long as you're careful and take her medication with you.'

'Of course. That way the house will be quiet, and you'll get to relax in that bath.'

'Wow, keep spoiling me like this and I'll come to expect it every day.'

He smiled and twirled his fork in his pasta.

Had she said too much? Assuming there would be an *every day*...?

It was hard not to talk that way, with how well everything was going between them. In fact, she couldn't remember the last time she'd been so content and so happy. Was it wrong to talk about what was going to happen between them? Perhaps she should just enjoy each day as it came and not push for anything? No point in tipping over the apple cart. She reminded herself to just enjoy the present, even if she *was* worried about how absorbed they were in each other as a small unit.

But this had happened with Simon. Was it a tendency of hers?

'You know what would go great with this? Wine.' Cole got up and opened a bottle of red.

She smiled as he poured some into her glass. 'Cheers!'

She finished her meal, mopping up her plate with the rest of the garlic bread. She really had been dreadfully hungry, and even managed a small bowl of chocolate mousse for pudding. Then, after a cup of tea, Cole put Tori in her buggy, ready to go out for their walk.

'When I get back I want to find you either in the bath,

relaxing, or fast asleep in bed,' he said, kissing her on the lips.

'Message received and understood.'

She yawned again and he laughed, kissing the tip of her nose. 'Go on, get up those stairs.'

'Yes, sir.' She laughed too, and gave him one last sultry kiss—it was to be their last one that day. 'I'll see you in the morning.'

Cole closed the front door behind him and happily pushed Tori's buggy ahead of him as they began their walk. This was his very first time out with Tori on his own and he was determined to enjoy every moment of it.

Of course, he hoped to have many more moments alone with her in the future, but today was the first. A novelty. A gift, showing that Lane trusted him to be alone with her. And he fully appreciated her trust in *him*, knowing how hard it was for her to let go and allow someone else to look after Tori.

It blew his mind how anyone could have treated her the way that man had. That Simon she'd known. He sounded awful. She was well shot of him.

'Da-da-da-da-da!'

Cole smiled at Tori. She'd only recently started saying this and he was so proud that he'd been there to hear it. 'Yes, sweetheart. Daddy. Look! Can you see the big doggy coming?'

A man was walking towards them with a giant-looking dog. He wasn't sure of a lot of dog breeds, but he knew this one was a Newfoundland. It looked like a giant shaggy bear. He nodded at the man, who nodded back as they passed.

Cole had never been so happy in his entire life! Out

with his daughter. Doing *daddy* things. Wasn't this what he'd always wanted in life? To be a doctor and to be a father? And now he had both. Life couldn't give him any more surprises.

He was settled and they were happy.

Lane woke with what felt like a cold brewing. She propped herself up in bed on one elbow and was aware of a scratchiness in her throat and a blocked nose and silently cursed at the inconvenience. But it wasn't surprising. She often found that when she started a new job—whether in a new doctors' surgery or on a new ward in a hospital—she would come down with something as she adjusted to the new germs that populated that area.

She slipped her feet into her slippers, grabbed her bathrobe and went downstairs to make herself some hot water and lemon...maybe take a paracetamol or two.

Cole joined her a few moments later.

'Sorry, did I wake you?' she asked.

'No, I was awake anyway. Have you got a cold?'

She blew her nose on a tissue. 'Yes—unfortunately.' She could hear it in her own voice. All blocked up and nasally.

'Typical. The one day I've got that safeguarding training and I won't be at the surgery to look after you.'

She pecked him on the cheek. 'It's just a cold. I can fight this myself—don't worry.'

'Just make sure you take it easy.'

She laughed. 'With a full day of appointments? Sure!'

He pulled her into his arms. 'I prescribe a full course of hugs and perhaps a foot-rub when you get home tonight.'

'I'll take that medicine, Doctor, thank you. Now, off you go! Get ready. Haven't you got to be there by nine?'

He sighed and reluctantly allowed himself to be pushed away. 'Yes. All right. But call me if you need anything.'

'Will do. Now, *go*!'

He left the house, and literally five minutes afterwards Lane did the same, so she could get Tori to her mum's house, so she could get to work. She didn't kiss Tori good-bye, not wanting to give her the cold, but instead blew her a kiss from the doorway.

When she got to work she was feeling decidedly snot-tier than earlier, and her body was beginning to ache, so she took paracetamol, washed down with some juice, and used a nasal inhaler she'd bought from a pharmacy on the way in. It helped to some degree, opening up her nasal passages and allowing her to breathe better. She'd just soldier on.

She called her first patient down. 'Gemma Rush, please.'

'Hi, thanks for seeing me so promptly,' said the woman. 'I've got to go to work in the next few minutes.'

'All right... So, you're here for a BP check?'

'Yes. I've been on the pill for a while and the doctor asked me to get it done, so...'

'Let me just get the blood pressure machine.' Lane got the equipment from a cupboard and set it down. 'Okay... Keep your feet flat on the floor and try not to speak. That can raise the numbers somewhat.'

'Okay.'

Lane turned to activate the blood pressure template on the system, so she could enter the results, and realised her head felt a little weird again. It had to be the cold. It couldn't be because she was tired—she'd slept so well last night.

The machine's cuff deflated and Gemma's readings appeared on the screen. They were very good. One twenty over seventy-two, which was perfect.

She showed Gemma, who smiled and rolled her sleeve back down. 'So I can carry on taking the pill, then?'

Lane nodded—then wished she hadn't.

'Are you okay?' asked her patient. 'You look a little… off.'

Lane laughed awkwardly. 'I'm fine. I'm meant to be taking care of *you*, not the other way around! It's just a cold—I'll be fine. You'd better get off to work.'

Gemma smiled, reassured. 'Okay, well—thanks again for seeing me so early.'

'No problem. Take care.'

Gemma left and the smile dropped from Lane's face. She really was beginning to feel rough. Light-headed and shivery and…

She decided to close the door to her room, needing a moment to take a breather, but when she stood up the room began to spin, and before she knew what was happening the world faded to black.

She was completely out of it by the time she hit the floor.

She didn't know how much time had passed, but when she began to blink her eyes open she was lying on her side, on the floor of her consultation room, and Mary and the other doctors were looking at her with concern.

'Oh, thank goodness! I knew you didn't look right when you came in. How are you feeling?' Mary asked.

Dr Summer had his hand on her wrist, feeling for her pulse, and Dr Green was slipping the blood pressure cuff over her other arm.

'I'm fine! Just a cold. I'm okay now.'

'You fainted.'

'It's this head cold.'

'Seems more like flu. Your temperature is sky-high. I want you to go home for the rest of the day and take it easy,' said Dr Summer.

'But I've got patients!'

She couldn't go home! She had a full clinic, and she knew how awful it would be for Mary to ring all those people and cancel their appointments, make them for another day.

'They'll understand. Can you get home safely?'

'I drove here.'

Dr Summer thought for a moment. 'I'll drive you back. It won't take me long—people will understand. You can pick your car up another time.'

'Okay…' He helped her to her feet. She felt a little woozy still, but better than before. 'But no one tell Cole.'

Mary shrugged and smiled. 'I'm afraid we already have…'

Cole was listening to the safeguarding leader, making notes as he liked to do, when a text popped onto his phone.

Please call the surgery.

He frowned a little. What could that be about? He would only be here for a couple of hours. What had happened that needed his attention? The other doctors were more than capable of sorting out any problems. Unless it was something personal…

His first thought was to worry about Tori. Had she been stung again? But if that was the case then the text would have come from Lane, surely?

Unless the problem was with Lane? Was she hurt?

The thought of that disturbed him greatly, and he had a flashback to what had happened with Andrea.

Lane hadn't seemed very well that morning. She'd said it was only a cold, but what if it was something else? His mind raced a mile a minute. She'd been sniffing a lot...

As his thoughts naturally went to the tragic, he recalled a hospital story of how a patient had thought he had a bad cold, and was sniffing, and it had turned out he was leaking brain fluid through his nose.

It was a million to one chance—but so was being killed in an avalanche. Or by a bee sting!

His panic caused him to hurry out of the training room, and with trembling fingers he dialled the surgery.

Mary answered. 'Oh, Dr Branagh. Thank you for calling so quickly.'

'What is it, Mary?'

'It's Lane. She fainted.'

His heart began to pound. He *knew* it! It was all about to go terribly wrong for him—as it always did!

'How is she?'

'She's okay. Dr Summer gave her a thorough check-up and then drove her home.'

'Right... Okay...'

'He thinks she has the flu, and maybe an ear infection.'

Okay. Dr Summer was a good doctor. Thorough. He trusted him implicitly. If he said Lane had the flu, then that was probably it.

But it still didn't stop him from being scared out of his wits.

'Okay. I've got about another hour here, but I'll give her a quick call. Thanks, Mary.'

'No problem, Dr Branagh.'

He ended the call and let out a big sigh. Okay. She was fine. But to faint like that…?

Had she eaten breakfast this morning? He hadn't seen her eat anything. She'd had a hot water and lemon drink, but that was hardly filling, was it? He ought to have a word with her about looking after herself better…worrying him like this. But maybe later, when she was much better. She'd be feeling bad enough as it was.

He dialled her home number and she picked up after a couple of rings.

'Cole. Hi. They told you?'

'Yes. Are you all right?'

'I'm fine. Just… It was silly, really, I didn't eat anything this morning—I didn't feel like it—and then I took some paracetamol and a nasal inhaler, and my head was thick, and I got a little giddy…'

'A little giddy?'

'I passed out. But I've forced down some toast now, and I'm sat in front of morning television—which is really quite dire, I might add—with my feet up and I'm doing nothing.'

'Good.' She sounded okay, but that didn't stop him from worrying.

'I feel bad, though. All those patients that have got cancelled—'

'They will understand perfectly. Don't worry about them. An ear syringing can wait a day or two.'

'But Mr Cilliers has his big dressing today, and—'

'One of the nurses can squeeze him in. He won't miss out. You just concentrate on you. Will you be all right for a little while longer? I've got to complete this training, and then I've got an afternoon clinic, but I could pop home at lunchtime to check on you?'

It occurred to him that he'd called her place *home*. Was that wrong? It had felt right, saying it. He'd spent more time there than at his own place recently. But perhaps all this was moving too fast? They'd only just started to get to know one another and they were practically living together, like a family, and…

Was that it? Was he mistaking the convenience of their situation for something more? Calling her place home… It *wasn't* his home. He had one of those. And this scare with Lane's health…what if it had been something terrible?

'You don't have to do that,' she said.

'I know, but I will. You keep watching dreadful TV and I'll see you later.'

She chuckled. 'All right. And I might have a snooze.'

'You do that. Bye.'

'Bye.'

He stared at his phone for a moment and then put it into his pocket. He really ought to get back inside, but he couldn't help worrying. She'd sounded fine, and it certainly did seem as if she'd just not eaten breakfast and then done too much. And if this head cold had given her an ear infection too…

He'd feel better once he saw her for himself—that was all it was.

He would think about everything else later.

Lane was woken by the sound of the front door closing and she realised she must have forgotten to lock it, before falling asleep. She pulled herself up to a better seating position.

What time is it? I'm ravenous!

'Lane?'

She smiled, hearing his voice. He was so good to her! He hadn't needed to come, yet he had.

'I'm in the lounge!'

'Well, stay there. I'm just going to get you something from the kitchen.'

She pointed the remote at the television, muting it, and then found another big smile emerging onto her face when Cole came in, bearing a tray with a hot bowl of soup on it, with a crusty bread roll, and a small curl of butter on a plate.

'Oh, Cole! You didn't have to go to so much trouble!'

He simply smiled.

The soup smelled delicious! 'Is it chicken?'

'Yes.'

'Where did you get it from?'

'There's a stall on Bourton High Street that does home-made soups, filled jacket potatoes—that kind of thing. I've been there before to get lunch when I've been out on home visits. The woman makes her own bread rolls, you know. Try it. It's sourdough.'

Lane pulled off a small hunk and took a bite. It was gorgeous! She dipped another piece into the soup. 'Aren't you eating, too?'

'I got enough for two. I just wanted to make sure you got yours first.'

He disappeared into the kitchen and came back with his own serving. He sat on the floor by the coffee table and they ate companionably in silence, until their bowls were empty and their tummies were full.

'You look pale,' he said.

'Do I?' He seemed upset by something. Was he worrying about her having passed out at work?

'Yes. You should be in bed.'

'I don't want to give in to it.'

'It's not giving in. It's being sensible. Will you do as I suggest?'

She looked at his face and nodded. He wanted the best for her, and perhaps he was struggling with what was going on between them, too? It had to be a lot for him to take in. Things had been moving so fast between them and he knew about what had happened between her and Simon. Did he think she was being the same way with him?

Everything was so uncertain. This taking-things-day-by-day lark was difficult when there were no certainties in life. And there were still all the legalities to sort out.

'I've called your mum. She's going to keep Tori until I can pick her up after work, and then I'm coming home to make you dinner.'

'I can do it. I'm quite capable.'

'I know you are. But you've had a bit of a scare today. So have I. And neither of us need any more of those, thank you very much. Let me make sure you're rested—you can come back to work when you feel better. Mary was quite frightened to find you like that.'

Oh. She'd not thought about that. Poor Mary. She would have to apologise to her, and also thank her for taking care of her so well. 'Fine. I'll go to bed.'

'Good.'

He stared at her for a moment and then stooped down to give her a kiss, holding her face in his hands. He looked deep into her eyes, his face serious once again. 'Don't you ever scare me like that again—do you hear?'

She nodded. 'I promise.'

CHAPTER TWELVE

THE NEXT WEEK was rough. Lane had continued to fight the flu, but she'd slowly begun to feel stronger under Cole's watchful eye. And when she was able to get back to work she went straight over to Mary and gave her a big hug.

'What's that for?' she asked.

'For looking after me. I'm sorry if I scared you.'

'Nonsense. I did what I had to do. Thank goodness for all that first aid training we have to do, right?'

Lane laughed and nodded. 'Comes in handy at times.'

Mary slipped her arm into Lane's. 'Now, come and have a look at what I've put in the kitchen.'

'Have you been baking again?'

'Choc chip muffins and lemon drizzle.'

'You spoil us, Mary.'

Now she was dealing with a patient whose ear syringing had been put off due to her fainting episode. She quite liked doing it. It was satisfying to get all that gunk out. She knew that sounded strange. Some people couldn't bear to see congealed wax. But she always felt a sense of achievement at giving back her patients the ability to hear better.

'Nearly done, Mrs Watkins.'

She had to take care and make sure she didn't injure

the tympanic membrane that was the inner eardrum with the small water jet.

'Good. I can't tell you how long I've waited for this. I was meant to have it done the week before, but it got postponed then, as well.'

'Did it? I'm sorry about that.'

'Wasn't your fault. I was booked in with the nurse but I had to go see my granddaughter—she was having one of her episodes.'

'Episodes?'

'She's always getting emotional. Calls me whenever there's a problem. She never really had her mum around so she comes to me, you know?'

She smiled. She understood. Skye had come to Lane about a lot of things. They'd had such a close relationship, and she'd felt privileged that Skye had trusted her with things that she couldn't tell anyone else.

You see? You had an intense relationship with Skye, too. You lock on to people. You don't give them space. That's why Cole has been odd with you these last few days.

Cole had been the perfect doctor to Lane whilst she'd had the flu, but since then she'd sensed a distance between them—a gap that was beginning to widen—and it frightened her. She felt a little hurt, too...

But she'd had a lot of time to think whilst she'd been ill in bed, and she'd realised that she'd contributed a lot to all the problems in her relationships by not saying how she truly felt. If things with Cole were to be different then perhaps she ought to tell him how she felt? That way he'd know where she was coming from.

'She thought she might be pregnant, but of course she wasn't.'

'How old is she?'

'Just eighteen—but we've kind of helped raise her, so we're very close. Her mum was useless, to be honest.'

Lane continued to squirt water—she was practically done. 'What made her think she was pregnant?'

'She felt sick. Tired. Apparently her monthly was late, but when we sat down with her she'd just counted wrong, that was all. Anyway, she's not—so the panic is over and I can get my ears done.'

'Well, it's good, that she wasn't. Unless she wanted to be, of course?'

'No, no. Her and her boyfriend have only been seeing each other a few months. It all got a bit too intense a bit too soon, that's all.'

Been there, done that.

She passed her patient a tissue and discarded the cardboard cup into the clinical waste bin. Then she went to put the machine in the sluice so she could clean it in a minute. She removed her gloves, washed her hands, and tapped the details of the procedure into the system.

'There we are, Mrs Watkins. All done until next time.'

She tried to smile. But she was still thinking about Cole. About Tori. About where they all stood.

Mrs Watkins gave her thanks and left, and Lane felt her shoulders sag when she was alone in the room again. She looked at the wall that separated her from Cole's room. They'd only known each other a few weeks and they were practically living together. They hadn't even spoken yet about arrangements for the future. Perhaps they should?

She loved him. But could she tell him? *Should* she?

Maybe it was all too soon and she was moving too fast. *Again.* Telling him how she felt would change everything, and if he didn't feel the same way then what?

She knew he cared for her. He'd looked after her so well whilst she'd been sick. But...

But she'd seen the doubt in his eyes.

Perhaps he was scared about what the future held, too? What if announcing her feelings would help *him*?

She kept trying to dismiss her doubts, but the more she fell in love with him the louder those voices were becoming.

If he rejected her it would break her heart in two. But wasn't it best to be honest? If he didn't reject her, if he felt the same way, then everything would be alright. It would be wonderful!

Lane looked at the purple fob watch that was pinned to her tunic. Ten minutes past ten. Six hours or so before work ended.

She had another patient waiting. A young girl of nineteen, who was there for spirometry with reversal to check and see if her breathing could be helped by using inhalers. Perfect. She could concentrate on that for a while.

Lane fetched the equipment and connected it to her computer. Then she called her patient in.

Cole had one last home visit to do before he could go home and put his feet up for the night. He was looking forward to that. He was exhausted! And he wanted a shower to wash away the cares of the day. It had been a long one. And it hadn't ended yet.

This patient didn't need treatment specifically. But she'd recently been diagnosed with a brain tumour and he wanted to pop in and see how she was. It seemed the right thing to do. He'd been looking after this patient for over five years, and remembered when she'd first come to him with chronic headaches, nausea and dizziness.

Deborah let him in and he wiped his feet. 'Hey, Debs, how are you doing?'

'I'm all right, Dr Branagh. You didn't need to come and see me at home—I could have come to you.'

'Oh, it's no problem at all. Kelvin home?' Kelvin was Deborah's husband.

She nodded. 'He's in the kitchen. Can I get you a cup of tea?'

'That'd be lovely. Thanks.'

She escorted him through to the kitchen and he shook Kelvin's hand and sat down, on their invitation, at the kitchen table.

'So what's the plan? Have you seen your consultant lately?'

She nodded. 'Chemotherapy will start in two weeks. It's going to be quite aggressive treatment, he said, and I should prepare myself for some bad side effects.'

'They can give you some meds to help alleviate those.'

'Yes, he mentioned I could have some steroids and some anti-nausea medication if I need it. I'm a little more worried about losing my hair.'

She ran her fingers through it, stroking it, smiling, and he could see she was trying to be brave.

'After that, if they can get the tumour to shrink a little, they said it'll be easier to remove with surgery.'

She was so young to have cancer. But then he guessed Skye had faced the same thing at a similar young age. Deborah had a little girl, too. Sienna. But she was older than Tori. About two years old, if he remembered correctly.

'You could try cold capping.'

'He mentioned that. I'll probably give it a go.'

'How's everyone taken the news?'

'Family's been good. We can't tell Sienna, though, she won't understand. But I wonder if…if you think I should make a will…just in case?'

A will. In case she died.

Another young woman whose life could be cut short. What was the universe trying to tell him?

'It's a sensible thing to do, but you must try and remain positive.'

'Oh, I will! But I just need to know that Sienna will be taken care of.'

He found it strange that he should be seated here, discussing her arrangements, when he hadn't been able to help Skye. It really began to sink in what she must have felt. What she must have feared losing.

He understood that fear. He couldn't imagine having to make that kind of decision himself, knowing he was to be a parent. Could he have done it? He'd given life a lot of thought whilst Lane had been ill, and his fears had been fed by the past.

Was he *meant* to be with Lane? He had very strong feelings for her—of course he did—but was it too much, too soon? He thought about her relationship with Simon, how she'd said it had been all-consuming. Well, didn't *they* have the very same thing going on right now? Was she feeling smothered? Because he thought that he might be. Not by her. But by the intensity of his feelings for her and what that meant.

He couldn't breathe sometimes because he worried so much.

He'd already lost everything once. Did he dare risk losing all he cared about again? Legally, he had no rights at all if he screwed this up between them.

Plus, he really wanted to spend more time alone with

Tori. Just the two of them. Could he apply to the court for parental responsibility? Discuss gaining formal access to Tori? He didn't think Lane would mind—after all, he was Tori's father.

It was great to be with Lane, working together to make Tori feel secure with him. But they were always together with her, and if Tori cried Lane comforted her, because she was used to being the one who responded. He needed the opportunity to learn what to do when Tori needed something.

He resolved to speak to Lane about that tonight. He had no idea what the future held for him and Lane, but he did know that he wanted a future for him and Tori.

She was his daughter and he would do anything for her. He would give his life, if need be.

Lane would understand that. She had recently been letting him take Tori out on his own, but that had just been for the occasional walk. He wanted to have a whole day on his own. A weekend, maybe? Lane might appreciate the rest! She'd been Tori's main carer for nearly a year, without a break and that had to be part of the reason she'd been so ill lately.

'It's good to plan,' he said now. 'You need to make sure your family will be okay.'

Deborah smiled at his approval.

He sipped his tea and watched as Sienna came running into the kitchen, trailing her blanket behind her. Deborah scooped her up into her arms and kissed her daughter's cheek.

His mind was made up. He would speak to Lane tonight.

Tori was splashing about, enjoying her bath, when Lane heard the front door open downstairs. She'd given him a key, trying not to make a big deal out of it.

'We're upstairs!' she called down, feeling her stomach churn and her heart pound even faster.

What was the best way to tell him? She was scared. Terrified. This was such a big step. But it was one she thought was the right thing to do. Tell Cole how invested she was in their relationship. He needed to know where he stood.

'Great. I'll be right up.'

She heard him put down his bag, drape his coat on a hook, and then his footsteps as he trotted up the stairs.

She gave him a big smile when he appeared in the bathroom doorway. 'Hey.'

'Hey, yourself. Anything for dinner?'

'We've had some chicken, veggies and rice. I put a plate for you in the microwave.'

'Thanks.'

She smiled at him, wondering how best and when the right time would be to start this conversation. The man had just come back from work. He'd had a long day, plus home visits to make. He was probably shattered. Probably best to leave the heavy relationship talk until after he'd had something to eat and a chance to clean himself up. It wasn't something that could just be blurted out.

'I've got this,' she said. 'You get something to eat.'

'You're sure?'

She nodded.

He smiled and headed back downstairs, and soon she heard him pottering about in the kitchen and the microwave being switched on.

She let out a pent-up breath and gazed at Tori. 'What do you think, Tori, hmm...? What will Daddy say?'

More than anything she realised she needed Cole! She loved him. But the last man she'd loved had left her. She

could be about to ruin everything they had. Their friendship. How well they got on. How good a little family unit
they were. She might mess all of that up by pressing her
own selfish issues!

But she needed to show him how serious she was about
what they had, and by affirming that, she hoped it would
show him that they could *do* this, live this life that they
were building and do it together.

She felt sure he felt the same way too. Didn't he act like
they were in a relationship? A serious one?

She scooped Tori from the bath, wrapping her in a
big fluffy towel and laying her on the floor to dry her
properly.

She could feel herself trembling. Her heart racing.

Tori giggled and Lane pulled her towards her, wrapping her not only in the towel but in a massive bear hug.
She closed her eyes. Soaking in this moment. This moment of near serenity.

Because she had to tell him. Had to let him know. She
couldn't live in limbo. She needed certainties.

And she hoped and prayed that he would say those
three words she longed to hear more than anything.

With Tori bathed and in her pyjamas, playing in her play-
pen, Lane straightened things in the kitchen and cleared
up in there. There wasn't much to do. Cole was very good
at tidying up after himself.

Looking around, she realised just how little of him
there was here. None of his things. No possessions. Did
he feel he didn't belong? Perhaps soon, when she'd spoken to him, he would feel better about everything? Bring
some more of his stuff over?

When there was absolutely nothing left for her to do

she went into the living room and sat down on the couch beside him.

He smiled at her and she reached out to take his hand. She squeezed it tight, taking a moment to just marvel at his strong hand entwined with hers, at the shape of his forearm, the chunky watch on his wrist. All the little details she loved about him.

'You okay?' he asked.

'Yep. I'm fine. Good. You?'

She thought he looked a little distracted—as if he had something on his mind.

'Yeah…'

'I…er…wonder if we could talk for a minute? If you're not too tired?' she said.

Now he looked at her. 'Sure.'

So this was it. Her big moment. And now it was here she found herself feeling nervous and wanting to giggle.

He locked eyes with her, still holding her hand. Still smiling. She hoped he would still be smiling when she told him how she felt.

'But can I tell you about what I've been wanting to say first?' he asked.

She nodded. 'Of course!'

'You and I have been getting on really well…' he began.

She beamed. *Yes*. They *had*. That was why this was such a perfect moment to tell him the truth about her feelings.

'And Tori and I have really got to know one another…'

'You have. And it's been beautiful to see.' She smiled.

'And you've let me take Tori out for a walk…that kind of thing. But… I want more, Lane. I need more than that.'

This was it. She could feel it! He was going to tell her

he loved her too, and then there would be kisses and hugs and laughter as they fell into each other's arms…

'When she was in hospital, it made me realise how—legally—I had no right to any of the information the doctor was giving us. If you hadn't been there I'd have known nothing. It made me feel…apart from you. Like an outsider.'

He wasn't, though. She'd been trying to show him that. That she could give him everything he wanted.

'So, I've been thinking really hard about this, and…'

She squeezed his hand tight, a big smile on her face, waiting to hear those three little words.

'I'd like to take Tori home with me for a while. For it to be just the two of us. I feel I really need to build that father-daughter relationship.'

Lane sucked in a breath, trying not to let her smile falter. But this *wasn't* what she'd been expecting!

He wanted to spend time alone with Tori?

'Just the two of you?' she said slowly.

He nodded. 'Yes. With your permission, obviously.'

She nodded hurriedly, still smiling, trying her best not to look as if she'd just been punched in the gut. Of *course* he would want some precious alone-time with Tori! Why *wouldn't* he? She was a wonderful little girl. He was her father. Of course she didn't mind! But it was hardly the declaration of love she'd hoped to hear. In fact, he seemed to be thinking about making plans that only included himself and his daughter.

I knew it! I knew I felt a distance growing between us!

But she didn't want to lose face in that moment. And in her heart she knew, he had a right to see more of Tori—no matter the legalities. He was her father. What was she?

'Of course, you can,' she said at last.

'I thought about taking her tonight. Getting her used to sleeping over at my place.'

His place. Of course. He wasn't thinking of uniting the three of them at all, was he?

'And I've thought about contacting a solicitor.'

Her face froze.

'To see if I can officially be named as her father. If I can be put on the birth certificate and apply for parental responsibility. Although I'm not sure on the legalities, to be honest.'

'You're thinking about applying for joint custody?' She stood there awkwardly, trying not to feel hurt, trying to seem as if she was open to his suggestions.

Cole frowned, shaking his head. 'I don't know… Maybe?'

'It sounds a great idea. Although it might take a while.'

'So you don't mind if I take her? It'll give you a rest for a while…after your illness.'

Lane couldn't bear to stand there a moment longer, her heart breaking in two, as Cole showed her very clearly that he was only thinking of a future with his daughter— not with her.

'I don't mind at all. In fact, now that you mention it, I *do* feel quite tired. Do you mind if I go to bed early? You know where her things are…'

'Are you okay?'

'Mmm-hmm.'

She turned tail and ran up the stairs, into her bedroom, and slammed the door. She flopped onto the bed and began to cry. She had known a distance had started growing between them…but for him to so cruelly state that all he wanted was to spend more time alone with his daughter! He wasn't thinking of *her* at all!

All that time she'd been sick with the flu she'd known something was wrong! Had he been too afraid to say it whilst she'd been sick? Had he been waiting for her to feel better so he could sideswipe her with his plans?

She froze, hearing his footsteps coming up the stairs. They stopped outside her bedroom door. She stared at it, awaiting the knock, but then she heard his footsteps once again, going back down. Him gathering things together. His voice, speaking soothingly to Tori. The front door, opening and closing.

They'd gone.

Both of them. She knew Tori would be fine. She was with her Dad! It was something, she knew that, eventually, she may have to come to get used to.

Cole sat in the soft play centre, watching Tori play in a ball pit for babies. She seemed fascinated by all the brightly coloured spheres around her, and was taking great joy in picking them up and trying to throw them.

He'd gone ahead and taken Tori from Lane's last night, but he felt terrible. Lane had *said* she was fine with him taking Tori on his own, but clearly she was upset. Was she feeling threatened by how close he was becoming to Tori?

She'd seemed her usual self lately, despite the flu. If anything, *he'd* been the one to try and create a distance. Had she picked up on that and thought he was looking to make a split? Simon had given her an ultimatum. Had she thought he was going to give her one, too?

He'd been up all night thinking about it, and his head felt thick with lack of sleep.

She really had seemed upset about him taking Tori. But surely she wasn't cross about his wanting to be an important figure in Tori's life? It was only right. He was her *father*!

He'd been happy to play their relationship Lane's way because he hadn't wanted to talk legalities right from the get-go. He hadn't wanted to upset his daughter, who clearly had a fabulous relationship with Lane. Lane was all Tori had ever known! But putting things on a legal footing had been more and more on his mind ever since Tori had got stung and ended up in hospital.

But now he was here, alone, and he wasn't going anywhere, and he didn't think there was anything wrong in wanting to know that Tori would reach up her arms for *him* when she wanted picking up. That when she cried, she would know she could go to *him* for comfort. That when she wanted to snuggle she could do so with *him*. That was what fathers did. They were there for their little girls. He didn't feel in the wrong for having asked for this part. He refused to feel guilty for it.

But…

But he and Lane had been getting so close, sleeping together, and he cared for her very much indeed. Of course he did!

But was it love?

He felt fear even *thinking* about it.

He'd loved a woman deeply before, and his loss of her had changed him as a person. Those early days and weeks after losing Andrea had been the worst days of his life.

Did he have the capacity to feel that way again? To risk his heart and put it out there?

Perhaps Lane had done him a favour? Life had given him a taste of what he could have and he'd been enjoying it, revelling in coming home to Tori and Lane, but had they been moving too fast? Perhaps involving a solicitor *was* a good idea, before it all got too complicated?

Cole knelt beside the ball pit and began to play catch with his daughter. She looked up at him with her beautiful blue eyes and laughed, and he knew he had Lane to thank for such a happy, contented daughter.

Was it his responsibility to make Lane happy and contented in return?

Had he been with her because of Tori?

Or had he been with her because he'd wanted to be? *Needed* to be?

The house was very empty without Tori or Cole. Lane had never actually been in her new home alone and it seemed very quiet. She had a whole weekend ahead of her before she expected Cole would be back. She knew she ought to use the time constructively, to get things done rather than moping around, but she couldn't because all she could think of was Tori and Cole.

The downstairs bathroom needs a deep clean.

That would take her mind off them, wouldn't it? If she made herself focus on inconsequential stuff like that?

Or she could go through her wardrobe and chuck out the stuff that no longer fitted, sort out the things she wanted to donate to the charity shop. Out with the old, in with the new. She had to accept the new …

She stood in front of her wardrobe and opened the door. Inside was a full-length mirror and she stared at her reflection.

She looked paler than usual, her face a little puffy, her eyes red with dark circles beneath. She wore an old tee shirt and a pair of jeans with a hole in the left knee.

How had she been so blind as to think that he might be falling in love with her, too?

Her talk with Cole had not gone the way she'd expected. And now he was out, alone with his daughter, which was apparently what he'd always truly wanted. Maybe he had cared for her a little, but it had not been love—and Lane knew she deserved to be loved. She would accept nothing less; she was worth more than a casual friendship with benefits.

The knowledge of that didn't stop her heart from aching, though. She loved Cole. Had allowed him into her broken heart and thought he was repairing it for her.

I always jump the gun. I always expect more from people than they're willing to give.

It was a fault of hers. A bad habit she would have to learn to break.

But there was no point in just standing here and staring at her reflection! She would do something useful!

So she reached into the wardrobe and grabbed a pile of clothes. If she was going to do this, then she was going to do it right!

'Dr Branagh!'

Cole was taking Tori for a walk through the park and who should be calling out to him but Mary, the receptionist from the surgery. She had a young dog on a leash. A golden retriever puppy.

'Mary! Hi, how are you?' He leant forward to give her a kiss on her cheek. 'And who's this little guy?'

'This little guy is a girl! Her name's Skylar and I'm out with her trying to get my ten thousand steps. I've got one of these thingamajigs...' she showed him the black strap around her wrist '...and it's been showing me that

I've only been doing around two thousand a day! Pathetic, isn't it? So, me and Bill got ourselves a puppy, to make ourselves get out and about more.'

He smiled and ruffled the dog's head. 'Good idea. Hello, Skylar.'

'Just you two out today? Where's Lane? At home with her feet up?'

He gave an unconvincing smile. 'Something like that...'

Tori squealed at the puppy excitedly, reaching forward to try and grab the dog's tail.

'Careful,' said Cole.

'Oh, Skylar's good with youngsters. She puts up with all my grand-kiddies chasing her about all day. Poor dog is pooped after their visits!' She looked at him, head tilted to one side. 'You okay? You look like death.'

'Thanks. I didn't sleep very well.'

'Tori keeping you up?'

No. Lane.

'Just couldn't sleep.'

'Well, that's to be expected, isn't it, with a baby? Lovely day, though! Get some fresh air into you—no doubt you'll sleep better tonight.'

'I hope so. I was just thinking about families and making memories. I'm thinking about taking more pictures.'

'That's a good idea! I could take some now for you, if you like! I'm a dab hand with a phone camera.'

'Would you mind?'

'Course not! Where shall we take them?'

'The flowers are in bloom by the bandstand—it'd be nice to get one done there, I think.'

Cole had wanted a photo of him and Tori for ages. He'd got some casual shots of Tori on his phone—ones that he'd snapped when he could—and of course there was the one of him, Lane and Tori dressed as faeries at the Faery Fayre.

He tried not to think back to that day. It had been so early in the relationship for all of them, but he'd thought they were happy. He'd thought he was doing the right thing, going at Lane's pace in his relationship with Tori, but he'd felt so much like an outsider at the hospital that time she'd got stung, and he'd just known he wanted to take further steps. Steps he'd hoped Lane would be happy for him to take. Hadn't she come here to find him?

He'd expected this to be a happy day. Just him and Tori in the park. But his heart just didn't feel in it.

Tori was in a pretty pink dress with a white cardigan, and Cole was wearing a blue shirt and jeans. He hefted her onto his hip and went and stood in front of the bandstand among all the roses. There didn't appear to be any bees today.

'What about here?'

'Okay.'

Mary stood in front of them and took shot after shot—some close-up, some panned back—and managed to take an absolute stunner when Tori randomly reached out to try and catch a butterfly that flew past.

'They're great.'

Cole smiled as Mary swiped through them afterwards, to show him. But though he smiled outwardly, inwardly he felt sad. It would have been nice to have got Lane in these photos, too... He was missing her terribly—something he hadn't expected to feel so keenly after just a few hours.

He looked at the pictures again. Did he really want pictures of just the two of them? Him and Tori? They were great. Absolutely they were. But someone was missing.

Had he hurt her feelings, asking for time alone with Tori? She'd seemed pretty shocked, even though she'd tried to hide it. But he loved his daughter, and he also loved…

His breath caught in his throat.

Love was what mattered.

And he knew he loved Lane!

Would she want to hear that?

I should have knocked on her bedroom door. I should have gone in. Explained.

He missed Lane like crazy.

He missed not having her with him. Her smile. Her laughter. The way she made him feel.

He wished more than anything in the world that he could tell her that he loved her…but he was too scared. If he announced it to the world—if he made it official— then…what? What did he fear would happen?

He'd opened his heart completely to Tori—why couldn't he do the same for Lane?

He thanked Mary for taking the pictures.

'Oh, no problem at all! Well, I'll let you get on. I've still got…' she looked at her gadget '…five thousand two hundred and seventy-one steps to do.'

'Mary?'

'Yes, love?'

'You and Bill… You've been together a long time?'

She nodded. 'Forty years next month. Never thought we'd get this far, to be honest. I could easily have killed him a few times!' She laughed.

'Was it ever scary?'

She looked at him carefully. Smiled. 'Of course! I'm often scared. Of loving him too much. Of losing him. You know he had that stroke a few years ago?'

Cole nodded.

'But I'm there because I love him. Because life without him is a horrible prospect. Because I want us to be together for as long as we can be.'

'But eventually something will happen, won't it? Life does that to us. Takes away those we love.' He thought of losing Lane and Tori, the way he'd lost Andrea and the baby. Could he face such losses again?

Mary fed Skylar a small treat from her pocket. 'Yes. But why deprive ourselves of the time we *do* have together? Of the one person who makes us happier than we could ever be alone? One year with Bill is better than no years with Bill. Now, I know what you're thinking, Dr Branagh…'

'Mary, I've told you before, call me Cole.'

She smiled. 'You loved Andrea, right?'

'Of course. But I lost her.'

'But you still have all those happy memories of her, don't you? Of the love you shared?'

He nodded.

'Imagine if you didn't even have that.' Mary raised an eyebrow. 'I'll leave you be now. Say hello to Lane for me. It's her last week next week, isn't it?'

Of course. He'd forgotten that. 'Yes.' Her last week. She would be leaving soon. If he told her he loved her, would she think he was only doing so to get her to stay? To not take his daughter away?

Mary smiled. 'It would be a damn shame to lose her.'

He nodded. 'Yes. It would….'

Lane had taken three bin bags full of clothes to the local charity shop and cleaned her house from top to bottom.

But all she could conclude from her efforts was that it sucked to be alone. More than sucked.

Her heart ached. She missed Tori so much, but she also missed Cole. He had become a part of her as much as her goddaughter had.

She hadn't realised just how much she had come to depend upon them being together. On having them in her life. It had only been one morning with them gone and already she felt their absence keenly.

All her life she had kept quiet when things got tough, and last night she had done the same thing again. She'd wanted to tell Cole how she felt, but she had silenced herself after his revelation about wanting more time alone with Tori. Yet again she had let other people steer her life for her, and she felt cowardly and angry at herself.

She'd never told Skye how she had truly felt about losing her. She'd never told Simon what a selfish man he was and how he ought to have more capacity for thinking about other people's feelings than his own.

She'd never got to tell her father how hurt she'd been that he'd left when she was little.

And so, when Cole had said how he'd like to take Tori home with him alone, she'd automatically caved and said that it was okay—zipped her lips about her own wants and needs.

Lane had had enough of other people making the decisions in her life. And as she stood there, looking at her clean and empty home, she resolved to tell Cole exactly how she felt. She was going to tell him off for messing with her heart. For making her fall in love with him and then breaking her heart in two. She didn't care if she made a fool of herself, because she was fed up with being silent and fed up with never telling people how she truly felt.

It might just be the most embarrassing thing she'd ever do—but to hell with it! She *would* be heard!

A light knock at her front door interrupted her thoughts. She really didn't feel like answering, and almost didn't. But then she thought it might be a delivery, and she was awaiting a parcel, so…

With heavy feet she traipsed downstairs and opened the front door—and instantly felt her heart begin to pound and her pulse start to race.

It was Cole.

And he stood there with Tori on one hip.

Tori squealed at seeing her and reached out. Lane couldn't help but smile at her baby girl as she took her in her arms. Couldn't Cole cope alone? Was that why he was back early?

'Is there a problem?' she asked.

'Yes. A huge problem.' Cole stared at her uncertainly.

'What is it?'

'You love her,' he said.

What was he going on about? 'Of *course* I do.'

'I know you do—and yet you just let me take her, like it was nothing. Something isn't right, and it's been bugging me, and it finally came to me. You gave her up as if it was simply something you'd have to get used to.'

'Well, that's what you want, isn't it? You and Tori to spend time alone?'

'Not in the way you believe. Yes, I want to spend time alone with her—I still think that's a good thing to do—but… But I'm getting side-tracked. I'm here to tell you that…'

She looked at him heart pounding. 'What?'

'Can I come in? I don't think I should say this on the doorstep.'

Against her better judgement she stepped back and let him in. It felt good to have Tori back home. It felt good to see him, too. She'd missed him, even though she hated to admit it, and it was difficult keeping up this front when all she wanted to do was tell him that she loved him, throw herself into his arms and feel safe again. The fact that she couldn't do that was making her sound curt.

In the living room, she put Tori down. She instantly crawled over to her box of toys and began dragging things out.

'So?' She stood opposite him, a coffee table between them.

'I *do* want alone time with Tori. It will be good for me, but I don't want to do it without knowing we can come home *to you*.'

She continued to stand there, arms folded, staring at him. She knew what she wanted to say. But clearly he still had plenty of talking to do, so she decided to stay silent and hear him out. Then she would say her piece.

'I'm her father, but you're her mother! We were a family the first day we met. I didn't know it, but we were. I tried to fight against it. I'm sure you did, too. But it happened anyway. I wasn't sure I could fall in love again. I wasn't sure I could be that brave. But you make me feel that way, Lane. You make me feel that anything is possible. That us being together is possible.'

Had she heard right? Had he said those words? Was he telling her that he loved her? This wasn't about Tori?

The thought made her heart race.

'What are you saying, exactly?'

She needed him to clarify. Because she had a bad history of getting these things wrong. Because right now she wanted to grab onto him and never let go—but if there was some small chance that this was still a rejection, then she didn't want to embarrass herself any further.

He smiled then, his eyes brightening. 'I'm saying I love you. I'm saying I have loved you for a long time and I want to go on loving you for the rest of my life. I'd like us to be the true family we are. I'd like you to marry me.'

Her heart was soaring. He loved her? He truly loved her?

'You love me?'

'Yes! I do.'

He came over to her, took her hands in his, lifted them to his mouth, kissed the insides of her wrists before holding them against his heart.

'I can't be without you. *We* can't be without you.'

'I thought that you…' She shook her head and sank against him, holding him tight. 'I thought I might lose you.'

'You'll never lose me. *Or* Tori.'

She sank into him, squeezed him tight. Grateful that she'd been so terribly, terribly wrong about him.

He pulled back to look into her eyes. 'Well? What do you say?'

She laughed. 'I'm saying… I love you, too. I'm saying yes to being a family.' She blushed. 'I'm saying yes to being your wife—if you'll have me, of course.'

He pulled her into his arms and kissed her like she'd never been kissed before.

She sank into his embrace, knowing that no matter what was to come she and Cole would be together for ever…

EPILOGUE

WHEN LANE WOKE she instantly turned to check on her baby. Lorelei had been born late last night, at three minutes to eleven, and had emerged into the world with a loud cry to announce her arrival.

Lane had looked into Cole's eyes and seen his tears, then she had pulled him close and they had hugged one another, crying, as the midwives cleaned up their newborn daughter before passing her over.

Lorelei was a beauty. But what baby wasn't?

Lane had been unable to stop looking at her all evening.

'You need to get some sleep. Both of you,' the midwife had said eventually.

So Cole had reluctantly gone home to catch a few winks and Lane had lain in the hospital bed, one eye on Lorelei's crib, as if she dared not look away in case her baby disappeared.

It had been a whirlwind of a pregnancy, but so much easier than she had thought. She'd had the usual uncomfortable symptoms, and she'd secretly worried that something might go wrong, but that fear had been lifted the moment she'd safely delivered Lorelei and held her baby girl in her arms. She was perfect. Ten tiny fingers and ten tiny toes.

Now Lane scooped her up and just sat there in the bed, holding her and looking down at her. Was it possible to love a human being so fiercely?

Yes, it was. She already knew it was.

She'd worried about that. She loved Tori so much, she had wondered if she would be able to love another to the same degree—but she realised now that the heart had an infinite capacity to love.

Loving another never took the love away from someone else. It just got more. It got bigger. Better than ever before.

Lorelei had Lane's nose and mouth, but her father's eyes, and she could already see the similarity between Tori and her new daughter. She liked that. Liked that there was a familiar trait. They were a family. Bigger than before, but so much better!

There was a gentle knock at the door and Cole peered around it. 'Ready for visitors?'

She smiled and nodded. 'You couldn't stay away?'

'How could I?'

He crept in, holding Tori's hand, and then scooped up his eldest daughter and put her on the bed, so she could see the baby.

'What do you think, Tori? This is your baby sister.'

Tori leaned in for a closer look, smiling. She hesitantly reached out and touched Lorelei's face, then leaned in further and kissed her on the cheek.

'Baby sister!' she said.

'Yes. Baby sister. This is Lorelei.'

'Lorry-bye!' Tori laughed and they all laughed with her. That was cute!

Cole draped his arm around Lane's shoulders. 'How are you feeling today?'

She let her head fall against his chest, then looked up at him and beamed a happy, contented smile his way. 'I feel as I always do when I'm with you. Like the luckiest person in the whole world.'

He kissed her, then kissed both his daughters. 'Not possible.' He smiled. 'That honour is all mine.'

* * * * *

LET'S TALK

Romance

For exclusive extracts, competitions
and special offers, find us online:

- **f** facebook.com/millsandboon
- **⊙** @millsandboonuk
- **𝕐** @millsandboon

Or get in touch on 0844 844 1351*

For all the latest titles coming soon,
visit millsandboon.co.uk/nextmonth

*Calls cost 7p per minute plus your phone company's price per
minute access charge

Want even more
ROMANCE?

Join our bookclub today!

'Mills & Boon books, the perfect way to escape for an hour or so.'

Miss W. Dyer

'Excellent service, promptly delivered and very good subscription choices.'

Miss A. Pearson

'You get fantastic special offers and the chance to get books before they hit the shops'

Mrs V. Hall